Gray Gold

Copyright 2016, Shawn D. Mahaney
Published by Stone Lake Historical,
An imprint of Stone Lake Press,
Seneca, SC, USA


ISBN 978-0-9963101-5-4 (paperback)
ISBN 978-0-9963101-6-1 (e-book)

Visit sdmahaney.org for more information,
discussion of the history around the book, and to
get updates on forthcoming works.

Waiting is not the same as doing nothing.

Doing nothing is something one can enjoy, even relish. Hell, the Buddhists even made it something to aspire to. Maybe if I ever figure out what they say about meditating, being able to think about nothing as well as do nothing, maybe then I can enjoy waiting too.

I was waiting all day, with everything to think about and nothing to do. Fort Selden used to be an important frontier outpost. The fort already didn't matter when they renamed Radium Springs, New Mexico, around it. Me with my car was the fort's entire garrison for that day, late in the spring of 1943. The barracks behind me consisted of a few lines of half-missing adobe walls, three feet high with plenty of gaps. It couldn't keep out a curious fox, let alone raiding Indians or banditos. The fort compound consisted of similar remains of several buildings, and nothing else. Modern developments in the town were mostly across the highway, closer to the Rio Grande, or to the north near the mildly radioactive local streams that drew 'health seekers' for many years.

The only entertainment there for me was a sign telling visitors how important the camp used to be, with an addendum below pointing out that Douglas MacArthur himself had lived here as a child. I wasn't counting, but after five hours waiting I started estimating how many times I had read the sign, involuntarily as I scanned the road for my appointment. I guessed it was about two hundred and forty-seven times when the truck pulled through the bar-less gate into the fort courtyard.

The flatbed truck was about as big as they come for an unarticulated vehicle. Its brakes gave several short squeals as the machine jerked to a halt thirty feet from my car. Three bulky bundles were tied down tightly to the bed under doped canvas tarps. The middle one was a squat cylinder, up on the round side. The other two were roughly seven foot cubes. They had told me I would be escorting important war materials. A bulge in the back tires of the truck told me it was about five tons of important war materials.

Fort Selden is just off the one main road through Radium Springs, which runs north from Las Cruces. The truck had come from the east, on a dusty minor road. The load was supposed to be imported, so I figured it came across from Mexico, though it could have come over Texas from a Gulf port. It wasn't something I cared about, it was just one of the many things I had plenty of time to think about during the drive ahead.

Another thing I had thought about was two dozen snarky things to say to whoever finally showed up. I was all worked up to let my very tardy date have it, in

2

spades. I looked up into the plain red cab at a paunchy middle-aged man.

"You need fuel?" I asked. "There's two stations on the main drag in town." I was more ready to get on with the job than to chew out some lackey driver.

The driver looked to his right for a second, turned back to me, and said, "We're supposed to go to the second one, north of here. Follow us."

I hadn't noticed the passenger at first. I waited by my car as the truck turned and pulled out. He was a small thin man, in a cheap summer suit coat and short brimmed dark hat. His features were so deep his face practically ran through him.

I took a long draw on my last cigarette of the wait and blew a lung full of smoke in with the dust kicked up by the departing truck. My motor fired up and two quick right turns had me north bound on the main highway. Less than two miles up I found the big red truck stopping at the outer pump of a two-island gas station. The attendant was on his way out to the truck before its brakes were set.

The attendant was an older fellow. I made him out to be the owner. Anyone younger than him by then had either been drafted or had gone into the city for top wages at a war factory. I parked next to the inner pump.

It was also getting late in the day for a gas station to be open anymore, with rationing in effect across the West for months. He had been expecting us, and was probably waiting around for the truck as long as me.

The truck driver helped himself to the pump while the attendant spoke a few words to the little man with the deep face. I went ahead and topped off my own twin tanks. As the meters quit singing, the attendant took a small pasteboard envelope from the thin man and walked back my way.

I held out a short stack of ration coupons as I reached for my wallet. He waved off both and bade us off. "It's all taken care of. You boys have a safe trip."

The old man shuffled off and the truck driver took his place in front of me. "Figured you might need this." He handed me a glass jug of water and a box of peanuts. "We got to stay on plan if you don't mind. We're already behind schedule."

I took the provisions. "So I noticed. Same route still?"

"Yep, no change," he shook his head. "We can catch a break in Arizona, but we got to keep going tonight." He looked off to the northwest, the way we were supposed to go, then turned back to me in an afterthought. "The name's Nicolas, right? I'm Sam if they didn't tell you."

"Nick will do, and yes, they did." I looked through him in the direction of our first leg. "We've got about two hours of daylight left. That should do us good until we have to turn west."

He caught my gaze and let go of whatever else he was going to say. "Alright, I know you been waiting all day." He was probably going to explain the delay. I knew the story would probably get better later. "OK, let's go," he said and promptly got his truck into gear.

Radium Springs went by in a dull blur. There was very little left of it. The last viable resort hotel was boarded up with fresh timber as we passed it. Radiation health spas had aged past fad status years before. Wartime vacation plans didn't often include such faraway dusty places, whatever the local attraction might be.

The lone restaurant left in town was closed by that time of day. Its few clientele would be workers from the nut orchards that comprised the one nearby industry still going. None of those people could be seen, already resting in their barracks from the day's labor. Only their impressive handiwork stood to declare their existence.

Their orchards had an almost supernatural order to them. Like on other farm lots, the plants came up at very regular intervals, so one can see rows form at different angles in passing. But those nut fields were also dead-level, so flat that the bounding berms, a mere two inches high, were enough to perfectly regulate the flood irrigation that was used. I knew there was more work to it, but the only obvious job once the field was laid out was to occasionally open a sluice gate on one of the little canals that catch at least one corner of every field.

On the way up from Las Cruces I had seen a few other crops, and many overbuilt homes, walled in that odd hybrid frontier-cum-Spanish-city fashion. The walls made the place look like a place, something deserving of a name cut into an ornate wood or iron sign on the main gate. But there was little real need for such a wall so far removed in time from frontier days, and so distant from the street criminals of a dirty old city.

In those houses I guessed lived the owners of the farms. The homes I saw in the evening, north of the orchards, were nothing but trailers or shacks, which had little ambience to gain from the golden evening sun. Their residents either worked the farms, or used to work in tourism and hadn't figured out yet what was next. A few of them with more land had some chickens or even a goat or horse.

It was easy to observe all this in detail as the truck I was following had settled into rigid compliance with the prevailing national speed limit. A poster at the gas station had declared, "Every mile you drive over 35 – Axis smiles!" For good measure the colorful placard included cartoons of the standard bad guys, including a wickedly taloned Nipponese general. I didn't dare think about how many hours the drive to California, along back roads, was going to take us at thirty-five miles an hour.

The job had come to me easily enough. I had moved to Tucson, Arizona, just a couple months before. After getting my bearings, and making a few reliable contacts, I placed an ad looking for security work. They needed security, from someone with a reliable vehicle.

Everyone knew about the shortage of rubber after war broke out with Japan. But just about everything else it takes to put on a good war took turns being scarce. A lot of those scare materials were assigned by government planners to new factories in the west. A lot of crooks took advantage.

If a load wasn't skimmed by men on the inside, it was stolen wholesale from a warehouse or on the road. Official prices on commodities were set by official boards in D.C., with four or five letter acronyms on their official letterhead. Street prices on things were set by whoever actually had the goods.

My ad had run in a newspaper with an editorial crying about the "Mexican bandit gangs raiding our highways!" I doubted they were Mexican, but the thieves probably didn't mind it being thought of that way.

The Zelatoff company had big contracts, with big dollar amounts on the eventual invoices, and needed all the materials it could get. They didn't want to use the main highways anymore, at least not near the border, or the usual rail town warehouses. Someone decided they needed escorts for their trucks.

Zelatoff had become a well-known name before the war, selling smaller and better radios than anyone else. They sold professional gear to the studios also. The immigrant son founder of the company was something of an American hero.

How they picked me I didn't know, but I had nothing else going. They offered more than I would have asked. I didn't even know they were going to cover gas.

The federal highway north from Radium Springs was paved and in good shape, just every now and then the road dipped to allow a stream to cross when flooding rains come. One of those sudden dips refocused my attention on the road, and on my car.

Before leaving New Jersey I had snapped up one of the last new cars available to civilians, a 1942 Lincoln Zephyr, "club coupe" V-12. It had what some thought of as an old-fashioned suspension. I knew it wasn't as smooth as other brands, but Henry Ford stuck with it because it still worked. It would get me through a long trip like this, over every kind of road, without worries of a fancy linkage coming apart.

I thought of some clever grade-school jokes on the name of the next town, Elephant Butte, far too clever for an actual school boy to come up with through his snickers. After there we would turn off the paved highway onto mostly dirt state roads. They were supposed to be recently graded, and I guessed they wouldn't have had much traffic. A full week fuel ration for most people wouldn't get them between gas stations across the high hills of the New Mexico desert.

On that point my car wasn't stock either. The original reason for installing two thirty gallon tanks where the back seat should be was to deal with gas rationing back east, which they started long before the west (ask any Texas rancher, who probably rents out plots for oil wells, if he thinks gas is actually in short supply in his neighborhood – when his neighbor is 20 miles away). Now that I was working in wide-open country, it was comforting to have range to blow by a gas station, that might or might not have gas, knowing I could go another two states before running dry.

Rolling along at thirty-five, if we can even call it rolling, I would have more range. I double checked that the pull bar to the carbs was yanked full out to maximum efficiency. The mechanic who installed it promised the engine would sip fuel like a nun at a whisky bar that way, but if I pushed it in, he had it set to open up wide and give me a good twenty horses over the stock setup.

After I'd bought that rig and tried it out, with a big grin showing, the greasy wrench showed me a bulletin about oiling problems on the aging Ford V-12 design. I was out another sixty bucks for him to fit a secondary oil pump, but I had a hot motor that could outrun and outlast anything on the road.

I'd made a few other changes to the car, but nothing that mattered on a simple escort job like this. All I had to do was keep the truck in front of me, and scare off anyone who approached it. I couldn't imagine anything getting in its way but a skittish road runner. But since I was technically on detail, I had a few appropriate tools.

The PI-standard snub-nose .38 revolver sat in its usual place, in a pocket holster locked in the glove box. I didn't like anything about it, but some places that license private investigators actually insist that a .38 revolver is the only piece they carry. Go figure. Anyway, it looks harmless enough that most people aren't put off by it.

More to my liking, and usually closer to me, was a Canadian-made 9 mm pistol. A lot of guys swear by the big fat .45 caliber rounds, but I had a baseball bat in the trunk which is about as useful for close-range slugging. Plus, when working alone I liked to bring a lot of friends with me, and the 9 mm stacks thirteen rounds under the barrel.

A classic Remington pump shotgun shared the trunk with the bat. It wasn't real smooth, partly because I'd notched parts of it to make more noise when racking. The noise of a shotgun being pumped is often enough to make a mob change its mind.

A little food and water, besides what the other driver had handed me, a good flashlight, and an overcoat for the desert night completed my kit.

I had maps, but just the kind they hand out at gas stations. With a little daylight left I checked our progress on the New Mexico map, which reminded me, *Paper is rationed – take good care of this map!*

A note near the map's Mexico border line warned, *Persons registered under Selective Service Act must obtain special permission from their local draft board before leaving United States.* We were heading

11

northwest up into the mountain plateaus of New Mexico by then. That's still the U.S.A. – it only looks like an alien planet.

## -3- April 13th (Tuesday); western New Mexico

The state highway climbed slowly through dull scrub land up from the Rio Grande. A small range of brush covered hills screened our eyes from the setting sun. It was well set once we made the last turn through the modestly winding pass. Only the faintest orange glow silhouetted the larger range that was another hour ahead of us.

By the time we started making turns through the higher pass it was completely dark. Just as the terrain became interesting, sightseeing was out of the question. I kept focus on the two red lamps ahead of me, setting up to turn in rhythm behind their moves left or right. There was only a low quarter moon and my own headlights to show me the road.

I stole a quick glance or two at the stars. The sky was clear and the deep view was something one doesn't get in the city any more. After just a few months in the southwest I'd grown accustomed to it though. The Milky Way and the millions of dots in and astride it would be there to look at for a long time after this drive was done.

The road was generally in good shape, even better than I expected. There was little to worry about, and the crux of the job became simply staying awake. Around ten o'clock I saw signs that we were in a national forest. The road got even better, through better maintenance and less use. I was glad, as it meant we were getting into more serious mountain switchbacks.

It became impossible to keep the truck in sight, not while keeping a following distance that would let me stop if they braked for a fallen tree or rock slide or such. But it wasn't like I needed to keep a close tail. There was no avenue from which the truck could be jumped, even if someone knew exactly where we were. And I wasn't going to make a wrong turn when there's only one road through.

Even mountain roads become monotonous after a while. Every time a turn comes, always in an uneven tempo from the previous two, a routine is repeated at the controls and in the driver's seat. I caught myself getting unnecessarily tense more than once, braced from clutch foot to a knot in my back as if I might need to spring into dynamic action in a flash.

It didn't help doing the run in the dark, after a long day standing around outside. I didn't know how dry the air was that day, but I wished I had drunk more water. It was near midnight when we finally broke through the last mountain ridge and sailed out into a smooth plateau.

Smooth here is a relative term. Dry river beds cut between branching runs of small hills the water had made between the larger mountains. It wasn't a flat plain with long sight lines, but it was soft enough that the highway was cut through or built up over the hills so we had only easy turns to make between long straights for the following couple hours.

Over a dozen hours removed from my last real meal, I took the chance to catch up on that count. I gave the truck some space ahead of my car as I reached back to find the stash of food and grab some water to drink.

The warm water was oddly sweet and refreshing. I knew then that I'd let myself get dried out too much. It took some discipline to think ahead and put the bottle down before guzzling the whole thing. I kept rooting around in the satchel I had behind the passenger seat until I found the box of nuts the other driver had given me. Once I had it open I could speed up again and remake contact with the truck. A crossroads was coming up and I wanted to be sure I followed the right way.

The truck was gone. Simply gone. It had vanished into the night, which by then was moonless.

I raced up the highway into a wide open flat that included the crossroads. Nothing was there to be seen in any direction. I had been too far behind the truck to still see any dust it might have kicked up. The crossroads was actually a confluence of three state highways, which meet in a wide triangle. I could see a long way down the road we were supposed to take, and down the other new highway, and both were dark

I had the presence of mind to stop short of the first intersection and get out. I could look for tracks in the

15

dirt, but only if I didn't drive all over them first. I left the engine running and headlights on bright as I got out with my flashlight to look around.

Crouching down to look at the road surface ahead, it dawned on me that I might have been able to hear the truck if I'd shut off my own car. But that opportunity was fading every second. I gave it up and looked over the road.

The road was recently graded, but not that day. Its hard dry surface gave only slight hints of tire impressions, and few small patches of tire tread pattern – not that I had thought to look at the treads of the truck I was tailing.

I drove slowly to the other corners of the triangular intersection. The highway didn't tell me much at any of them. Yes, a few trucks had come through in the last day or two, but I couldn't pin any of the marks on my truck.

I also found the beginnings of multiple dirt tracks running off away from the main highways. Stopping to put a light down some of them, I thought a few could possibly take a heavy truck. I was in no position to explore down unmapped desert trails by myself in the middle of the night.

Reducing the possible courses of action to two, I looked at the map by flashlight, while smoking a leisurely cigarette. There wasn't anything to hurry up about now. I could either go back, or keep on driving to where we were supposed to go. I figured going to the end was the most direct way to let whoever at my employer needed to know what they needed to know.

I allowed myself another big slug of water, as I expected the next leg of the trip to go a bit faster. Pre-war speed limits were not going to impact my itinerary, let alone the new thirty-five.

I drove all night to make the original rendezvous, near the main rail yard south of Phoenix, Arizona. There was no direct way, and the mountains in between were more stubborn than what I'd just driven, but I could relax and let my car do what it was made for.

I blew past the touristy trinket shops at the edge of the great Apache reservation. I cut cleanly through the last mountain pass and came down into the city with a bright sunrise behind me.

I put in a few gallons of gas at the edge of town, not too much lest someone get curious, and picked up a local map. The attendant saw my "C" grade gas ration sticker, took the appropriate stamps from me, and made change without any questions.

The ration board which had set me up for fuel had me down as some kind of clergy man. I thought maybe I needed to decide what denomination in case it ever came up.

Phoenix being a clean all-grid city, I had no trouble finding the address. The city was going about its weekday morning business, sparse traffic moving easily.

The appointed place turned out to be a new car dealer. Of course it wasn't anymore – there was no such thing as a new car to sell anyone. A dealer with a good garage could keep up service business, if he could get parts. Some stayed afloat trading used cars, but even that market was tightening up.

I waited for a few Army trucks to pass so I could turn left into the empty front parking lot. I didn't see a soul. I parked at the outside edge of the lot, backing in so I could watch the building.

I had just keyed off my engine when a door to one side of the empty showroom opened and a medium height brown haired man in gray coveralls leaned out to wave at me. He got my attention and pointed me toward a bay door a few feet down from him. I restarted the Lincoln and motored to the door as the man went back inside to roll it up.

I pulled in and parked on the flat concrete. It wasn't a full working garage; it was a simple shop where they used to prep cars for sale and do light jobs. Another overhead door on the far wall allowed for through traffic. I figured it was all just long enough to park three cars inside, or one truck like the one I was supposed to have brought with me.

I shut off my car again and got out. The whole way in I hadn't really been able to decide how I was going to tell the story to whoever I met first. I certainly didn't know what kind of reception I would get.

The brown haired man was sitting with a shorter heavier man off to the left, up a step in the former customer waiting area. They sat at a set of a table and four chairs. A stacked deck of cards and a few neatly

18

folded sections of newspaper shared the table top with three coffee mugs.

I was waved over to come and sit down with them. I walked that way to go and sit down with them.

The shorter man spoke up first, before I reached the table. "This fellah looks a little lost. What do you think, Harvey?"

The man in coveralls addressed me directly. "You do seem to be missing something. What can you tell us about that?"

I sat down in the chair opposite him, with my back to the vehicle bay. "I'll tell you all there is to tell, but who am I talking to?"

"You want to be sure of yourself. OK." He leaned forward a little. "My name is Harvey. Your name is Nicolas. You were hired by the Zelatoff company to escort a flatbed truck to this location. The truck had a red cab. Does that all sound right?"

"That's right so far." I took off my jacket, letting it drape open over the chair behind me.

"And I'm Miles," offered the shorter man, "only they call me Smiles, on account of my jokes, I guess." He smiled without any inference. "Say, Harvey, this one seems pretty smart, dontcha think?"

20

"Sure Smiles. Why don't you go call in and see what Nick here is supposed to do next, OK?" Smiles got up, leaving his light gray jacket laid over the back of his chair. Harvey and I both watched him turn down a hallway out of sight. I proceeded to tell Harvey about my night.

He listened quietly. He did not ask any questions until I finished. "How far back did you say you were when the truck 'vanished'?"

"At the rate we were going, I might have let it get a half mile ahead of me before I got on the gas again to catch up. Even if they'd floored it at just the right time, that truck couldn't have been more than a mile up when I got into the open flat." I caught myself hammering the table with a pointed finger for emphasis before we were interrupted.

Smiles came back out, barely five minutes after he had left, cradling three coffee cups in an unpracticed manner. He announced without segue, "He said he's supposed to go on ahead."

Harvey parsed the pronouns faster than I could. "You should go from here to the main office. Mr. Thompson there will want to hear about this himself. You can get paid today if you make it there in time to catch him."

I downed the coffee quickly and thanked the two men as I got into my car which they let out the rear bay door. Paid? I started the day just hoping not to get arrested!

They had given me an address in Palm Springs, California, and said I should ask for mister Nigel Thompson. I checked the map's mileage table while trying to drive. With the time zone change I had plenty of time to get to the far side of Palm Springs during business hours. 24 hours removed from a hot meal, I looked for a place to eat.

On the north side of the state highway just outside of Phoenix stood a place called "Ma's Diner." It was perfectly predictable, which was exactly what I needed. 'Ma' was a burly hirsute man in a white t-shirt and blue apron, working the grills behind the counter. A plump waitress in snug gingham uniform dress gave me my pick of seat, as the morning regulars were all gone, save two old-timers sipping coffee at the west window, out of the morning sun.

I sat at the counter and told Ma what I wanted, and to keep my coffee mug full. The coffee was insipidly weak and as he poured the second cup I asked if a pot could be brewed that wasn't fit for schoolgirls on a sleepover. He pointed at a sign declaring "Two Cup Limit" and asked, "Dontcha know coffee is rationed now?"

I reached into a pocket to fish out two full silver dollars which I slid across the counter. "Yes, and it is also price controlled." I drank two deep cups of rich dark inspiration with my breakfast before I bid my new mama goodbye.

After sitting for a bit, and waking up a little, I thought back on all the things I'd missed back at the garage. Harvey and Smiles might not have known much, but I never even tried to talk around the edges of it with them.

I wasn't the first chump to lose a truck on his way to meet them, and it may not have been the first to simply vanish. I hadn't even thought to note and remember any details about the two men. Harvey might be my age, but might be ten years younger. Smiles was enough of a character that I let everything else about him get by me completely. Somebody must like him though.

I hustled through more desert and more mountains, stopping only for water for me and for the car. I got a little gas, though I probably had 35 gallons on board. I had sunglasses on against the last afternoon light when I turned in to Palm Springs. I hadn't been there before, but this was not a sightseeing trip. I cut directly through town to the factory.

I found the address with no mistake. The Zelatoff building had swallowed up all the 900 through 1600 address blocks on its street. It was enormous, especially compared to the many low small houses and shops I passed to get there.

The office portion was a full height block on the end of the long factory building. It was impressive by itself. I drug my tired feet up the steps to the main entrance, found the receptionist, and asked for Mr. Thompson, giving my name.

A few minutes later, Nigel Thompson met me in the lobby and took me into a small adjoining room.

"Please sit down, Nick. My name's Nigel." He carried a slight accent, like from one of the old immigrant boroughs of New York. It might have been Irish two generations ago, and it made his familiar tone alright.

He was maybe fifty years old with a solid angular face under combed light hair. The face didn't reveal any disturbance from having heard my story.

"So you didn't go down any other branches of the crossroads? Oh, yes, that's perfectly understandable. I don't much see what you could have done either." He seemed only keen to reassure me. "We don't really think putting out one man to escort a truck is effective security, but we have to appease our current customers, you understand."

"Oh, is it a military contract requirement now?" I hesitated to ask questions which might prolong the conversation, but my curiosity doesn't shut up easily.

"No, not quite that." Mr. Thompson grinned a little. "They do expect us to take care of the materials that are released to us, but we know not all are going to make it to the end. An independent escort might stop some theft, but it gives us a witness at least."

Before I could ask anything else he pulled a single sheet of paper from a drawer in front of him and pushed it over the table to me. Only then did I notice the smallness of the little meeting room, filled up by an old office desk and two chairs.

"I got some details of your story over the phone ahead of you and had it written up. If you could sign at

24

the bottom, I will run off copies to satisfy the state police and whatever new bureaucrats the production boards anoint to bother us. I'll make sure you aren't troubled about it after today." He added quickly, "I also had your check printed. It's waiting in another office."

I wasn't keen on being drawn into whatever they had going on, but this seemed like the cleanest way out of it in any case. At a glance the statement did match what I'd said happened. And on the other end of my signature was an appointment with a hotel bed. I signed.

I followed Mr. Thompson's directions through a door behind the receptionist, left down a hall, and into a caged space on the right marked, "Mail Room." I approached a short counter with a not overly young blonde behind it. She looked up and as an introduction asked, "You Nick Guyon? I swear, they had me drop everything to get you a check cut. It's been sitting here for an hour and I'm not even finished with this morning's mail."

Her abruptness barely diminished the fact that her voice was the most pleasant thing I'd heard in days. "Yes, I'm the fellow who turned your day inside out. And I'm terribly sorry! Now, may I ask who it is that I inconvenienced just to get myself a little pocket money?"

She looked at me sideways for a second then turned and smiled directly my way. "My name's Anne. Just Anne." She extended an arm with a thin envelope in its hand.

I left the arm hanging a moment. "Very well, Anne. I am Nicolas, or just Nick. I do some special security work for the company. I have some other jobs going, but if I get back here again, can I ask them to have you draw up the check?"

I finally took the check so she could reclaim her arm. "You can ask, and they just might." She smiled impishly.

I said good evening as pleasantly as I knew how and exited out a side door to find my car. By failing dusk light I scribbled all I could remember into a notebook. I took special care in recording every detail under, "Anne, Mail Room."

## -5- April 15<sup>th</sup> (Thursday), Palm Springs, CA

I drove way out of town, south through the Coachella Valley. I felt like I needed to put some distance between me and the Zelatoff company. I needed a hot shower and a cool bed, but I didn't even try to look for a room in Palm Springs. It wouldn't have mattered if I did want to stay there. Between the new Army air bases and people coming to work for Zelatoff, every hotel was probably booked up and most boarding houses double bunked men who work opposite shifts.

I rolled along the east shore of the Salton Sea. The sun inched ever lower into the gold painted water as I passed. It began to look warm and inviting. It took some effort not to turn my car out onto the beach so I could feel for myself if the water had turned into warm candy.

The crossroads town of Brawley, California, had the fortune of being too small in 1940 to get the attention of any industrial magnates or military planners. It had the rare privilege of continuing largely as it was – a way post for seasonal farm workers or weary motorists. I got a room with no trouble.

By meager parking lot pole lamp and the last of the evening sun I unloaded my car into the dusty roadside motel. This involved my coat, my guns (I don't like leaving them in the car if I can help it), and what was left of my stale food. I expected it was too late to find a restaurant open, so I dined on dried beef and peanuts with warm tap water.

I finally opened the envelope from Zelatoff. At a hundred and twenty dollars, the check was generous for two day's driving, even supplying my own car. It was drawn on a San Diego bank. I'd have to get back to Tucson to cash it where somebody knew me.

I slept like a rock, at the bottom of the ocean, with a sunken battleship on top of it.

The only window of my small room faced north. It was nine a.m. before enough daylight snuck in around the curtain to wake me. I showered, putting the same clothes back on when I was done. (Yes, a good private detective would always have a couple changes of outfit in his car. But I reminded myself that I had been on a simple security detail, so I didn't feel too low about myself.)

I traded the room key for directions to a good breakfast joint, and ate my fill at another example of the Great American Diner. I don't think any other country has or will have such a gold standard for simple independent restaurants. The coffee was better at this one and I only got a single scolding finger from the waitress as she poured my third cup.

It was seven or eight hours back to Tucson, which I'd lately called home base. With this last job done, I thought about what I wanted to do next. Thoughts like that as often as not lead back to what one has already done.

I had followed my father into the Detroit police force after a year and a half of college. His family never approved of his marriage and my mother had no local family. The police force was our family.

I probably got into more than a young beat cop would normally be expected to see, but the old salts trusted me. One of them told me I'd probably make my choice of sergeant or detective by age twenty-five. Prohibition made the choice for me. I didn't see how an honest cop could get by in a border city, except by redefining "honest."

So I went to New Jersey and hung my own shingle for private jobs, on the ocean coast well away from the shiny new Canadian distilleries.

As an ex-cop I knew less than nothing about the private investigator biz. As a P.I., I couldn't flash a badge to get answers out of anyone. I couldn't leave a stakeout to let some rookie take over on the graveyard shift. I didn't know how to get clients either, and took some lousy jobs for a while until I got some wealthy regulars.

I was wrong about getting away from the smugglers, too. The Jersey shore was thick with them. Big ships would lay off shore and little speed boats would run booze right into the big cities. It was more direct that driving the stuff from Niagara or Miami – with fewer middlemen to pay off.

I did the usual jealous husband and missing teenager cases, but I got into a lot more, sometimes even helping out the state and local police when they had their hands full (which was always). Then when some clean cut kid turned up dead and his rich old Aunt Gertie couldn't imagine her nephew being mixed up with gangsters, I had to chase down the gangsters.

Fingering gangsters for murder is touchy business. If I could give Aunt Gertie a suitable placating story, and bank a favor from the ruling mob, I figured everybody was better off.

Along the way I'd met a circus tent of shady characters. Some of them preferred to be known in polite company as respectable civic leaders. If I dug up something on one of them along the way, and it wasn't anything to my client at the time, I'd let them go on looking clean and added it to my ledger of favors owed.

I kept pretty busy in my dozen-plus years on the east coast, too busy to spend what I made. Between private detective work and a few odd jobs I had built up a pretty good bankroll. Late in 1942 I read the winds and decided the American west was the current land of opportunity.

Tucson, Arizona, had looked like a good place to stick my map pin. It was not too big a place to get a handle on. The war had not torn up the business sector in the city, outside of keeping the large downtown rail yard busy for three shifts. To feed my sort of business,

30

the city had a good mix of old money with established interests and young blood to agitate them.

The Army Air Corps had thought to put a regular air base in Tucson, serving its position as a national border outpost, and several training fields, to take advantage of the stubbornly clear weather. I appreciated the second point myself, with forty-plus gray wet winters under my galoshes.

I had taken a small monthly motel cottage south of downtown, put half my savings in a local bank, and set about learning the town.

Tucson locals were keen to talk about local history, and could point to where many bits of that history got paved over. Ghost stories were popular. I guess even a steam roller can't flatten a troubled spirit.

Tucked between the Santa Cruz River and its Arroyo Chico tributary, which had been doubled up by a major highway and a two-way rail line respectively, downtown Tucson was compact and tall for a western town. A pair of eight story buildings had bragging rights over several blocks of smaller towers. Beyond either river the city was just many more acres of comfortable sprawl. Steep mountain tops supported the sky in most directions, but there were miles of flat basin in between.

I started out pounding the pavement downtown. I would need an Arizona private investigator license, but there was no rush. I had no real jobs and wasn't looking for any yet. If some rich maniac stumbled upon me and threw cash at me to go find his cat's lost jewel-studded collar, I would just have to take the case and ask for forgiveness later.

The downtown restaurants and clubs I found full of mid-level businessmen and bankers who thought they were a cut above. I didn't bother to remind the bankers that their entire existence consisted of taking a six percent cut of what those businessmen built (or taking a bath if the loans never came back). Fancy parties at the Rialto or the Pioneer Hotel might have been good places to meet some even more inflated townies, but I had no invites and wasn't ready to be gate-crashing during my first weeks in town.

I was more at home in saloons over by the expansive rail yard. Some evenings it was a reunion of old scoundrels from back east, on both sides of the law. Michael "Mickey" Salazzo said he gave up rum running on the Atlantic a full year before prohibition ended. He got hired on by a railroad and managed to get himself a coveted stationary job there in Tucson. He said he was even thinking of starting a real family. I wondered if he'd divorced either of the women he was supposed to have been married to on either end of Edison, New Jersey.

Skirting the northern edge of Tucson I found a mutt-ly mix of local tradesmen, contractors, CPAs, grocers, teachers, and the similarly dissimilar. There I ran into my own shadow. Young Merrick Folton had followed in my own footsteps, joining the Newark, New Jersey, police department after his father. In '41 he had left to work for one of the copper mines in Arizona. The mine wanted protection from union organizers, who were grabbing their share of the new American west along with everyone else.

Most bars and clubs I tried had their own distinct flavor of clientele, who seemed to like it that way. The one place I found to be a true democratic forum was the Randolph Park Gun Club, a quasi-municipal facility in the south east corner of the city. When talking calibers and trigger pull and headspace, every man was equal. If a fellow's opinion differed from yours, be he a gangster or cop or rancher or accountant, he was an idiot until he outshot you. (Then you wanted to know everything about his rig.)

That was where I met Arthur Mason.

Professor Mason was retired from teaching history at the University of Arizona. Technically he had been an 'adjunct lecturer,' not a professor, but everybody called him Professor. He was also retired from being a reserve police officer, selling life insurance, roofing contracting, running a moving company, and of course he had published three books on local history (including the ghost stories). His version of retirement meant joining the rural district volunteer fire department and taking up gunsmithing as a profitable hobby. He also had connections who could get us ammunition for civilian use.

I got to know Professor Arthur pretty well. It was deliberate at first, once I saw how connected the guy was. I had him work over my lousy little .38 revolver, which I had never wanted and never liked. Once he was done with it, I was finally happy with the feel of the action – clean and easy but sure and crisp. I got a friendly history lesson on compact side arms along with it, and couldn't help but share some of my own experiences under that topic. I had made a friend.

That night coming back into town from California I didn't care to go out anywhere. I ate dinner at a small neighborhood place, picked up the last two days of local newspapers, and retired to my little motel cottage.

-6- April 16<sup>th</sup> (Friday), Tucson, AZ

I woke a little before eight. Once I was clean and dressed I walked around the next building and across the main parking lot to the motel office. Tracy at the desk told me I didn't have any messages and asked again if I was ever going to get a real office. I tapped the newspapers folded under my arm and said that was exactly what I planned to work on that day.

The morning sun was warm on the back of my clean blue shirt as I walked across the highway to our local breakfast counter. I took one of the few small tables by the long street front window. The usual waitress took my usual order. The eggs looked a little small and the bacon strips a little short, but it was an open secret that the government had simply redefined terms like "prime" and "large" after locking up all the top grade food stocks for military needs.

I skimmed the main headline stories while eating. Fighting in north Africa. Fighting in the Solomons. Federal intervention in another strike.

Over a cigarette and second cup of coffee I got into my usual chore of working through the inside pages. A kitchen fire with no casualties but loss of the entire house. A war bond event coming up. A war bond event total from two days ago. A boring weather forecast.

I took my time over the classifieds. I wasn't in the market, but used car ads said much about conditions in any city. At the beginning of rubber rationing, every car ad claimed 'good new tires' if it could. Very few made the claim any more. It was a cinch that the wheels of the cars available now were shod in ratty old shoes. The lucky ones would have gummy cheap retreads, which were at least partly new.

As I came across space-for-rent listings, I circled some and took a few notes. I needed a more permanent place to live, and a small office would be OK if it could be had cheaply enough. Just into the last paper, the Tucson Citizen afternoon edition from the day before, a short story jumped out at me.

Prominent in section B, on the front page under the fold, was the headline "Another War Truck Hijacked on NM Highways." The article mentioned the Zelatoff company, that it was a critically needed load of copper wire and plate, and that the entire vehicle was taken. Thankfully my name wasn't mentioned, just that, "a hired armed escort was overcome entirely by the brigands and did not even observe the direction of their escape." I thought it was a hatchet job, but I wasn't about to call in and complain.

Of course the whole episode still irked me, but I was determined to keep a forward focus. I walked back home to get my hat and coat, got in the car, and went out to drive by some of the places I'd marked in the want ads.

I looked at the downtown addresses first. I skipped the places that turned out to be just a room-in-a-house. That left pricey tower apartments. Tucson wasn't overrun like the war factory towns, but middle-ground accommodations were pretty well soaked up by families of workers from the expanding air bases. I parked and walked around a few blocks of downtown anyway. I had done this before, but not with an eye toward having to live there.

I had never liked dense urban centers, where a brutish building can put the whole next block into shade. I liked parking by my own door, to bring in groceries I could cook myself. I knew people figured out how to get these things done in a built-up city center, but I guess I'd never been motivated enough to figure it out for myself. Tucson was certainly not as dense as Jersey City or Manhattan, but its downtown was close enough and I'd never cared to dwell for long in those boroughs.

After forty minutes of circular wandering downtown I found my car again and cut under the railroad tracks into the loose suburban sprawl that made up the rest of Tucson. The city proper didn't even threaten to meet the foothills of the mountains that dominate the northern view. I checked a couple spots outside the city, where development was unevenly sparse. One developer might have put six houses on one parcel, with new streets around them, but the next three blocks were unpaved with just two or three campers on rented corner lots.

Inside city limits I looked at a place that turned out to be a trailer behind a commercial shop. A few others were drive-up apartments, but hardly different from the motel I had been in for several months. A tidy two bedroom house, south of the university and backing onto a city park, wouldn't be vacant until the end of May but was already signed for when I got there.

Lunch time found me in the southeast part of the city. I pulled into the expansive grounds of the El Conquistador resort hotel. I drove around the main building to park near the big pool. They ran a bar back there which overlooked the pool and the first of many courtyards between the various buildings.

I was not surprised to find professor Arthur there, as they called him something of a regular at lunch time. He shook my hand at the bar and suggested we get a table. I followed him to a quiet corner of the room, away from any other part of the sparse crowd. We each had water and a beer in front of us and food orders off with a waitress when he started to talk shop.

"Tough luck about that escort job. That was a lot of metal to see go, wasn't it?"

"Wait, what? You mean the Zelatoff truck in the paper?" I put my beer down without having taken the next sip. "Why are you asking me anything about it?"

"Come on, Nick. Don't you remember you told me a week ago you had picked up a security job in New Mexico for Tuesday? I did see the bit in the newspaper, and don't think you P.I.s are the only ones who can put two-and-two together."

I had forgotten telling him about it. I caught up with that sip of beer. "OK, yep, that was me. But don't think for a second it went down like in the paper."

We paused a moment for a cup of soup to be set in front of the professor. He gripped a spoon while declaring, "I've been around long enough to know better. The news story was fed to the paper; I could only guess by who."

"We'll I couldn't even guess at who either, if that's what you're fishing for." I fumbled for my pack of cigarettes. "I'd just as soon forget the whole thing, but it sure was too weird for any quick forgetting."

Professor Arthur kept at his soup, looking straight at me with his spoon clamped in his lips. I had managed to get a cigarette lit, pausing to heat it up with a long draw as I decided if I would indulge his expectation. "OK, fine, I'll tell you how it happened," and I did just that.

My food came and I found the cigarette in my hand half burned with a long ash precariously ready to fall from it. I crushed it out and got my own silverware busy as Professor Arthur came up with a few questions about the story over the course of the meal.

"You say the moon was gone, but it was a clear sky, right? Just two guys in the truck? No, I don't have any idea where to go with it all, just trying to line up any facts that might matter." I believed him, but I couldn't help but feel that he already had some notions.

"Do you think I need to dig into this? Are you hiring me for the job? I didn't think so. Look, I've already been paid, they want the case closed, and so that's how I intend to keep it." I hacked off a too-large piece of tough steak, holding it in the air as I emphasized, "I need to get a practice going here, you know."

"Yes, of course you do." The professor smiled patronizingly. "But if you did get it figured out, you could have quite a magic act going! '*Presto magnifico*, watch this building disappear!'" He chuckled softly at his own humor as I shook my head.

The teasing over, we finished up talking about guns and women and other more important things than life-and-death business. I left to finish my tasks for the day, leaving the professor to do whatever retired guys who've seen and done it all do on a sunny Friday afternoon.

I didn't actually have any other business for the day. I did have a mood to fix. I didn't know the word then, but you could call it 'pensive.' I went back downtown to get out and walk around some more. It seemed smart to be around people but not actually with anyone. Downtowns are good for that.

A few blocks into my pacing I wandered into the Plaza theater. The afternoon block of shorts promised to be all comedy, followed by an Abbot and Costello feature I hadn't seen. Very little seemed funny to me. I didn't stay long enough for "Pardon My Sarong" to get interesting.

I found my car and went a roundabout way to the north, just feeling the gears shift and motor hum. Eventually I parked near a cluster of shops just west of the university. It was a nice area, clean and well built up, without being  over done or uppity. A big college will do that, as students and faculty bring in outside money to spend, from parents and from the state. I hung out around there often.

A good number of other non-university locals that I knew would also take advantage of the area. Some of them were natives, others recent transplants like myself. At my first stop I came across one George Fusaro. George had been working as a mechanic in Philadelphia when I was doing gumshoe work out of New Jersey. (Out of habit I looked him up through a contact back east and word was he did a lot of wrenching for bootleggers' fast cars and boat motors back in those days.)

The narrow restaurant was lightly occupied, faculty largely gone home and students not gone out yet. A long bar ran down the left side, eight tables along the right. George was sitting with another fellow at the dark bar and gave me a nod in passing as I found a seat further down. He kept talking to the other man for a couple minutes then came to say hi. "Hey there, Nick. Howyadoin? Any trucks up and vanish on you today?"

I didn't flinch at his remark. I took a slow sip of my drink before I turned toward him. "I guess word gets around quick around here. But you know the grapevine likes to dress things up to make a good story. Where'd you hear that line about a truck vanishing?"

"Oh, Nick, you know how it goes. One fellow says something, three other guys hear it, six different stories get spread around. Don't you worry about it. Say, you gonna let me look at that car of yours any time?"

"I'll keep you in mind if anything ever goes wrong with it. You got a lead on tires in the size it needs?" I stole a glance down the bar toward George's previous companion.

George was trying to get the attention of the bartender for another drink, not looking at me when he answered, "I'm still working on that, but I'll keep you in mind, too, OK?"

"Fair enough. Say, who was that guy you were talking to a minute ago?"

"Oh, I don't know, Harry something maybe, just met." George turned to look back that direction. "Well shoot, he's gone already or I'd introduce you."

"I'm sure Harry-something is a swell guy. When you were talking, did anything about disappearing trucks happen to come up?" I looked at George over the rim of my glass as he squirmed a little.

"Well, um, yeah, I guess that might have come up." He leaned farther over the bar trying to catch some ray of observance from the bartender. "Look, Nick, you gonna stay a bit? I'll get the next round."

"No, I have some work I still need to get done tonight. Catch you next time."

I went back to my car to recover whatever newspapers and sheets of notes I had saved from the last few days. I walked another couple blocks up to a bigger restaurant, in a small cluster of larger business buildings. It had a better after-work crowd, but that was thinning out. I took a table by the street facing window, almost in the far corner from the main door and the small bar. I got a quick bite to eat, opened up my papers, and got to work.

She sat down at my table unannounced. I pulled my papers in closer to me to make room for the watered-down beer she set down in front of her. "I hear you're a private eye, hot on a case, and looking for help. Mister... Guyon, is it?" I didn't ask where she'd heard. The bartender there would dish out anything, and make it up if he didn't know, for either a two-bit piece or a wink from a charming young blonde. This little lady had not had to pass any quarters over the bar.

Miss Carolyn Barnes was from somewhere well east, had little reason to trust anyone, was younger than me by ten or fifteen years, and was looking for work. I found out these things mostly by inference, as she wasn't readily telling me much of anything about herself. Truth was, I did need help.

I gripped my pen in a loose fist on top of my note pad, sipping my drink as she talked. "I signed up for a detective course not too long ago, you know." I did know there were a lot of 'trade schools' popping up lately, some of them actually legit. "It looked like a solid program, didn't promise to be a pushover – two hundred hours of class time, plus field work." She downed a major fraction of her fractional beer. "They only asked for half the first month's tuition down."

"How many hours of instruction did you actually get?" I brought up my own drink for a sip without looking down.

"None! Well one, if you count the hour I spent crying over the fifty bucks I was out. That counts as a lesson."

"It certainly does," I affirmed. "I'd bet fifty bucks it hurt more getting swindled than losing the cash." I took another sip just to hide my grin at her expense.

She turned to look up to her right, out through the window at the three story building across the street. "I hope you don't always bet that easily. I've got two kids upstairs waiting on me, and they need fed every day, whether their mama's got fifty bucks or nothing."

I had been in that building on my first trip through Tucson, months before. "Is Mrs. Torge running a hotel over there now?" I'd gathered that the old lady would let her building out for whatever brought in the most cash that week. It was something besides a hotel during my previous patronage.

"Not really a hotel, but rooms are available and we have a private bathroom. She's got the whole top floor set up for monthly rent, no transients. She told me she does daycare, but I don't think she ever thought of it until I walked up with those two."

45

The young woman was looking pretty sharp. It had taken me longer to figure out Mrs. Marilyn Torge, who had been left one of the few tall buildings outside of downtown Tucson by her late husband. She was hard to miss around town, from church bond rallies to 'morality league' meetings, her ample girth was a dominating presence. Once I got to know a few of the more reliable disreputable local characters, I got the gist of her reputation. She had her fingers in more than Sunday bake sales.

It was getting near dark and I still had no plan for the next day, but I knew well how I could use an attractive, assertive, worldly young woman. The conversation turned to the practicalities of me having an associate and what she might have to do. Details of trade craft would wait, but she would have to be able to lie like at least a five-dollar swindler. Danger wasn't mentioned, nor was salary.

When her beer was finished she set it down somewhat loudly at the end of the table. The floor server noticed and came to check on us. I asked for another round for both of us, on my bill, which I was ready to pay.

Carolyn took the cue to bring up money. "So, this job you're on, we're on, is it paying any expenses in advance?" she finally asked.

I squared up the situation for her. "To tell the naked truth, I'm not on a job. I'm pretty sure I got played for a fool on the last job though, and it's given me a serious itch. I'm going to figure it out for sure, but

I can't expect there's any pot of gold at the end, let alone pocket money for the trip." I laid out a weekly wage and per diem setup which she nodded was OK.

She caught herself glancing back up to her apartment, quickly turning back to face the empty chair next to me. "I've got to make arrangements here before we leave. Is mid-morning tomorrow OK?" I said it would be and she left me to finish getting nothing out of my notes.

I was met the next morning in the street, at one minute before the appointed time. Carolyn had one small suitcase and one large purse, accessories to a fresh new dress and neat little white hat with fake lilac flowers (I have no idea what lilacs looks like, but the flowers were sort of light-purple-ish, and I call those lilacs.) Her hair was done up in a way that must have a name, and her makeup was modest but precise. She could have been going to church instead of on the road with a scruffy stranger. I didn't know her well enough then to notice the tiredness in her eyes and rasp in her voice.

I handed her a small roll of bills. "We'll be at this not less than a week, so I'm going to front you half a week's salary. I know you had to get the kids set up with someone and Mrs. Torge is not likely to babysit on credit."

"Oh, no, she understood completely, she..." Carolyn inhaled heavily and covered her mount with the back of her clutching fist. She turned away from me and looked up toward the sky, breathing twice slowly to recompose herself. After a short minute she dropped her arm, turned her head downward for a moment, and turned back toward me with a calm, cold face. "The kids are all set. Are we ready to go?"

## -8- April 18th (Sunday), Arizona highways

It was quiet in the car for the first half hour. It would take most of the day to get to Palm Springs, moving at a rough approximation of the new national speed limit. I didn't get up to more than double the limit, even in the open desert.

I broke the silence. "Can you use a camera?" I asked Carolyn.

"If you mean, 'do I know what all the dials and little numbers mean,' then yes, I do. In fact, I used to have a pretty nice Argus. But that got sold last year."

There was more to the story, but I let it go. "Carolyn... Do people call you Carol?"

"They do. And I *hate* it. Please..."

"Alright, alright. Ca-ro-lyn, it is then," I exaggerated all three syllables. Something shorter would come up once I knew this woman well enough to drop a nickname.

Of course at this point I barely knew her, and was going out on an odd sort of case with her, just like that.

But I wasn't worried – nothing I had in mind hinged on her coming through. And, if I worked it right, even if she messed up, nothing would come back on me. If she did well it could be a big help. If not, I could cut her loose with a bus ticket back to Tucson.

Without prompting or asking, Carolyn turned on the radio and started looking for something to listen to. I didn't mind. The only reason I hadn't turned it on myself is that I knew there was nothing on. Watching her intently adjust the dial, slowly up and down thrice through the entire range was as much of a show as anything to be found on air.

On that Sunday morning we heard Kate Smith start into God Bless America for the ten thousandth time. A local preacher had harsh words for our sins. One droning newscaster was talking through weekly price lists of commodities that matter in the region. A distant signal carried static-accented Mexican traditional music.

One bright spot came when Dinah Shore sang the last half of "Skylark" for us. But that station was fading and neither of us could make out anything of the next song. Carolyn bet me if it was a man or a woman singing, but I couldn't tell and could never check on it to settle the bet anyway.

She asked if we would have to stop for gas any time soon. I explained about the oversize fuel tanks, and a bunch of other things about the car, before I realized she was really asking about getting a restroom break.

At a crossroads oasis outside of Gila Bend I pulled in and put a dozen gallons of gasoline into the Lincoln.

Carolyn went inside for a few minutes. After I cleaned the car windows, I went in too. When I came out she was standing in front of the touristy knick-knack shop next door to the service station. She was holding a small fanciful statue, a multi-colored ceramic snail with a bouncy metal spring for a neck.

"Something for the kids?" I asked.

She didn't look up. "The boy might get a kick out of this, and they are letting stuff go pretty cheap." She tipped up the hanging paper price tag one more time. "But, he needs new shoes first." She put the trinket down. "Are we all set?"

I handed her a cold soda bottle. "Yes. Let's go."

We continued on through the Arizona countryside without incident. A hot wind picked up, driving dust and debris in the air. Rain clouds menaced in the mirror but never caught us.

Somewhere near the California border Carolyn gave a gasp as I hit the brakes hard. The hot drums drug us down to a quasi-legal speed after a marked police car came into focus on the horizon.

It was a false alarm on my part. The cruiser was parked off to the right side of the road. Its officer was standing some ways up, talking to an old man next to an even older small truck. The old man was gesticulating slowly, pointing to objects on the ground and at a freshly cut gap in the straight barbed wire fence that bordered the road for miles.

We drove by slowly, slower than strictly necessary. Carolyn covered her mouth, though it was closed and silent, at what she saw. Decapitated heads of cattle were strewn in disorder to either side of a neater row of piles of bovine entrails. I couldn't count while driving, but it had to be over two dozen.

"Thirty-one," Carolyn said in a cracking low voice.

"You counted??" I asked, incredulous but curious.

"What? Oh, yeah. Old habit. I pick up useless details." She turned to me to ask, "But what was that all about?"

"First of all, please do hang on to that habit, at least for the next few days. Secondly, it's all about beef."

"You mean like cattle rustlers? Used to be they walked off the herd whole on its feet."

"Exactly. After lopping off the head and forelimbs and other junk a cow is half the weight to haul off. They'll bait them to a spot on the fence, then come one night to cut it, do a roadside slaughter, and take the carcasses god-knows-where for butchering. They'll sell the best cuts for double the government price, with nothing into it."

She turned around to look back at the scene. "I feel so bad for that old rancher..."

"Bad? Dearie, he's probably in on it! He'll still clear good money per head through the bandits, and might even have an insurance policy to cash in – if that cop plays along."

We were mostly quiet for the rest of the trip.

It was nearly dusk when the fringes of Palm Springs could be seen through my dusty windshield. I had called ahead to reserve space at a nicer hotel, well across town from the Zelatoff building. I wanted to avoid us being seen by company people if I could help it.

"This is where we'll stay for tonight. Tomorrow we'll start you on what we talked about." I picked up her small bag from the trunk and explained, "We will have to share a room. A mixed couple traveling separately would be a little too odd." Only then I realized I hadn't asked if the room had one bed or two.

It turned out that the Hotel del Tahquitz was frequented to a large extent by men from the Army air field east of the city. Two years before the town was thick with Hollywood playboys instead of itinerant flyboys. We found our second story room in the rear of the main building. As a 'suite,' it had a short half-height wall separating the small sofa from the two beds. But it had a balcony which overlooked the pool, where several young men were roughhousing like grade school boys. I had half a mind to drop all my plans and join them.

Instead I told Carolyn, "Give me just a minute to get cleaned up and I'll go get us a table for dinner." The sink and vanity of the room was in an alcove with no door. The toilet and tub were paired together in a separate room. I made quick work of washing my face and running a wet comb twice through my dusty hair. I grabbed my jacket, pausing at the door to ask, "How long will you need to get ready?"

Carolyn was already at the sink with a small paper sack of necessities. She looked at me sideways. "I will be right behind you. I don't know who else you've had to wait on getting ready, but it certainly wasn't me."

I took that to mean at least twenty minutes. She found me at the bar in five. I could see she had touched up her modest makeup, but I couldn't tell you in what way exactly. I looked her up and down summarily. The hat was gone, her hair was fixed up differently, and she had put a crème colored jacket over the pastel dress. I hadn't even talked to the restaurant host yet, having just got a cold drink in my hand.

"You didn't believe me, did you?" she asked, her face not betraying any smugness.

"Quite honestly, yes, I did believe you. But if I were a betting man, and I am, I'd have to bet on experience over faith." She took the comment with a half-smile. I put two dollars on the bar for my drink. "Let's find us a table."

The restaurant was pretty busy, with several officer's uniforms holding court. The host said reservations had booked up the only open tables and reminded us that it was a weekend evening. Except people hardly had weekends then, with every war plant or third-string government sub-contractor working six and seven days a week. I got my nose into his reservation book and pointed out a party of four that was already twelve minutes late. That and five dollars got us seated at a larger table than the manager would have wanted for a couple.

Carolyn waited for my lead when the time came to order drinks and food. I was hungry and thirsty and I led the way with no vagueness about it. I thought it might have been a long while since her last multi-course meal.

Conversation came around to how each of us got there, it being all we had in common. I took my story all the way back to my parents in Detroit, father from an old French family and mother a second- generation Greek orphan (or maybe a bastard, I never did get the straight story).

I got interrupted a few times with questions about the detective business when I talked about my Jersey days. I assured her she'd learn all about it if she stuck around. At that time our focus was the one job.

For her part she talked mostly about the previous two years, which had been hard. As a single mother, she wanted to both be with and provide for her children. The world would not permit both.

She had married the father of her youngest child (her boy was seven, the girl four) and followed him away from her western Maryland family to West Virginia coal country. His two hundred fifty dollar life insurance policy didn't last long, even with generous help from the mine ladies' league.

She couldn't get in the door for work at any of the newly unionized companies. Other places were firm about needing full-time 48-hours-a-week help, with starting pay that would barely cover child care. She picked up small jobs during school hours, sometimes waiting tables at night when a neighbor could be counted on to check in on the kids at bed time.

She had packed up and come west on word that the new factory towns were being built up with lots of different opportunities for all situations. The papers had spilled buckets of ink over Henry Kaiser's giant day care centers.

They stopped in East St. Louis for a while, camping in fields like most of the other sudden transplants. Not seeing when that was going to get any better, she deduced that Tucson might be better off, for the same reasons I had.

"Don't we need to talk about the case, what you plan to do next?" she finally asked.

"That's what we've been talking about all day, the whole getting-to-know-you routine. The plan as it stands isn't much more than to get as much information as we can and improvise from there. When we're winging it, we'll have to each rely on the other to play along and act in a predictable way."

That got a genuine smile from her. She soaked in the presumptive partnership for a minute, chewing a bite, before admitting, "It's just that, with all this 'getting-to-know-you' stuff it almost seems like a date."

"If this was a date I wouldn't have told you half of what I just did." I looked down to stab a piece of mid-grade steak, "And you're the one who's been playing a close hand."

She set down the fork and had the heels of both hands on the table edge. "What do you mean by that? I'm just who I am, and you can ask me anything about it." She sat up straight and took on that increasingly familiar cold face.

"OK then. What's the mailing address of the father of your first child? What county even?" I didn't look up until after I'd finished the question.

Her face walked through six or seven different bare emotions before she squared it up again at me. "Has anyone every told you that you're a miserable rotten bastard?"

I said with my mouth half full, "Yes, in fact I almost married her despite that. Or because of it, I'm still not sure." I finished chewing and continued, "I didn't say it wasn't fair. You're the one taking a bigger leap of faith tagging along on this trip. You probably should be the one feeling me out."

She fidgeted in her seat a little, not quite starting to get up, before settling in to finish her meal. I outlined what our plan was for the next day, getting affirmative nods along the way. She almost wasn't mad at me any more when she went up to the room ahead of me to get dressed for bed.

## -9- April 19<sup>th</sup> (Monday), Palm Springs, CA

Carolyn Barnes woke just before me. She rose quietly and began getting ready for the day while I laid there with one eye open. She picked out clothes, showered, dressed, and finished getting ready with some measure of indifference to my presence. While combing out her damp hair she walked over to my bed. "How long have you been awake? I tried to be quiet."

I sat up a little, propped up on a folded pillow. "Just a little while. No need to worry about me. You'll have the place to yourself soon if everything works out anyway."

She smiled. "I'll try to take care of the place. No wild parties while daddy's away, of course!" She laughed at her own joke and I smiled back. "So, did I dress all right?"

She wore a simple blue dress in a rough weave with a flat belt over black flat shoes and dark socks. I said it was perfect for the day's job. I threw the covers back and got myself out of the bed, ready to be un-swaddled from the long pajamas that I didn't usually wear.

Carolyn asked, "What time do we have to get going?"

"There's no particular schedule," I explained as I scratched just a few of my itches, "but it would be best for appearances if we got you to the factory in the morning."

"OK, if there's time I was going to sit by the pool for a while." She was packing a handbag for the day.

"Plenty of time. And why don't you see if we can get food served there, and coffee. I'll find you there." I replaced her at the sink to unpack my own kit.

I also showered but put on the same suit from the day before. I had no appearances to make. Carolyn timed it perfectly and a mug of hot coffee was served just as I got to her table outside. The morning desert air was chilling and the sun had not yet cleared the main building to light the inner courtyard.

We ate a light breakfast and headed for the car. I grabbed a copy of the local bus schedule in the hotel lobby and handed it to Carolyn in the car. "Fold this over a few times and rough it up some, like you've been carrying it around and using it for a while."

I drove us directly to the Zelatoff factory, right up the main drag where the glossy hotels had drawn a steady train of playboys and starlets until barely a year before. Now most had signs out front advertising to servicemen.

We circled the factory slowly. I pointed out where she would go in to apply for work. The hopeful part of the plan was to get Carolyn hired in the office area, where she could snoop around. Short of that, there were a few particular things she was to ask about, without being too obvious about it.

I drove halfway back across Palm Springs while Carolyn studied the bus routes. We picked a stop that would get her a northbound bus. She would connect in the north part of the city to a route that went to the plant. I left her a block from the stop and started my own tour.

I zig-zagged through the city blocks until I hit what had been the northern edge of Palm Springs before the war. Here was the new 'boom town,' the same as it was in most other places that welcomed new war factories.

A few rows of cheap dormitory buildings took up one block, the city's first attempt to accommodate the new war workers. After that everything was improvised. Some larger private parcels were managed camp grounds, neat rows of sites with communal facilities of some sort. But much of the great camp was completely unorganized, people scattered to wherever they simply decided to park their old car or overstuffed backpack.

A few families had decent tow-behind campers set up. Many people lived in tents, some of them built to last a while, others meant only for the occasional weekend in a state park. Improvised lean-tos and tarp shelters appeared in amazing variety, between those showing skill and resourcefulness and those that were pathetic reflections of their desperate owners.

That Monday morning most of the occupants were gone. I saw only a few women and children moving about. It was miserably hot and finding airy shade was the only goal in life for most. One woman I distinctly noticed was sitting beside a beat up old car. The car had at least two flats and hadn't moved in a good while. Tarps were tied to the rear and the far side of the car, making a simple shelter. The woman sat in a cheap folding chair in a faded pink dress. She faced the road, emotionless as the hot breeze tossed the strands of her greasy hair that weren't tied back. It took me some time to realize that the wadded-up blanket over her left arm was a breastfeeding child.

Most war plants paid over-the-odds for labor, and Zelatoff paid better than most. But money can only buy what someone else has to sell. No industrialist was ready to commit to building out a whole private city for workers when the previous generation of them had been publicly crucified for running company towns (with company stores, company banks, company laundries, etc.). People here were served by a motley assortment of vendors with carts or cheap shacks that could be moved or abandoned when the inevitable time came.

Municipalities couldn't just print money to make developments materialize, or the water and sewer plants to serve them. Federal grants didn't make the needed steel or concrete fall from the sky either. Camps like this one quickly got at least a little bit of ad hoc organization, so water wells were not right next to a neighbor's pit latrines.

Some private developers happily built new apartments, but some questioned the investment remembering how the last war ended suddenly just a year into the big American mobilization. A few fat cats were able to cash in on the 'great war,' but a lot of small time investors were out their entire capital if not deep in debt. Palm Springs already had a happy speculative market in modernist homes before the war. The modularity of those designs was being tested as multiple families were being wedged into each of them.

None of this was news to me. I'd seen the same thing in other places. My tour that morning had a practical purpose. I needed to find a place for Carolyn to stay in Palm Springs, actually or plausibly, if she managed to get in at Zelatoff.

I wasn't optimistic about finding anything worth looking at (I had some standards of cleanliness and safety for where I might have to leave her), but I had nothing else to do for the day. If I didn't find a place, she'd have to stay at the hotel across town. She would need a cover story in any case, as specific but unverifiable as possible.

Vacant camp sites were advertised on crude signs that had become the dominant local weed. Most of them were nothing but a naked patch of California. A couple of simple boarding houses claimed to have space, but the only one I walked into was all men, some of them hot-bunking the same bed to save rent.

I might have found something if I kept at it, but the truth is I was resigned from the start for this to be an expensive adventure. Carolyn would stay in the suite at the Hotel del Tahquitz. To get back to Zelatoff she would take two or three buses every morning, walking a way between stops, to break up her route. For her back story I picked a cheap motel closer to the air bases, a place where it looked like a new kid in town could live anonymously for a while.

That settled I drove back to the start of her morning bus trip. A donut shop there had both cold ice cream and a window from which I could see the bus stop. There was no reason to expect anyone to be tailing her. There was no reason to expect her to notice if someone was.

I saw her get off when the bus came. She walked half a block the wrong direction then stopped and turned around abruptly. She scanned the street behind her before making a show of checking the time and looking up something on her worn-looking bus map. Only then did she walk back and come into the donut shop, ordering at the counter before casually running into me like it was a chance encounter of acquaintances.

She was going to do just fine at my sort of work.

"OK, where'd you learn all that?" I asked as she set a small sundae glass on the table across from me.

"Learn what?" she replied coyly before pursing her lips tightly around the small metal spoon. I waited for a better answer. "OK, well, I do read some, you know. Not just stories; I read some serious how-to stuff before I tried that detectives' course."

I couldn't complain, but felt like I had to say something to keep mastery of my new apprentice. "Sure. That's good – but don't forget that you're going out on zero field experience. I'm not going to stick you anywhere you should need more tools than I've checked you out on myself. Got it?"

She sat up straight and gave a stiff little salute. "Yes, sir, understood sir! Private Bimbo first class reporting sir." She dropped the salute and focused on her ice cream again. "I won't go on being smart any more than required. Sir."

If I were her age, I would have rolled my eyes in exasperation. All I did was let it go with a tight lipped sigh. "Look, just... you're doing fine." I rubbed my forehead where my hat band had sat all morning. "How did it go today?"

"I don't have a job." She finished the last bit of her ice cream and put the spoon down on a paper napkin. "They said the office was fully staffed. If I wanted a job in the factory I could have started training right then. Training is two weeks, with deferred pay until working for real another two weeks.

"I acted all dainty and broke. I said I didn't think I was cut out for real work, and did they really not get paid for a whole month at first?" Carolyn made a ridiculous face while quoting herself about being 'not cut out for real work'.

"OK, that's all what I expected. How about the rest of it?" I asked, not even realizing that I was leaning in closer.

"I'm getting to that," she said with a slow-down hand gesture. "I nosed around a bit while taking my time filling out paper work. The folks there are plenty busy, and they'll sure tell you about it, just to have someone to complain to. Like anybody, I guess.

"So here's what you asked about. The factory people get paid weekly, every Friday. The office staff get paid on the first and third Tuesday of every month. Those that like to go out hang around a couple of the hotel bars on the main strip."

I glanced at my watch to check the date, counting back two weeks. "So payday is tomorrow, right?"

"Sure is," Carolyn nodded, "and they were all happy about it, talking about plans for a good paycheck when rent isn't due right away. Oh, and I met a woman named Anne, might have been the one you told me about."

I definitely leaned in at that mention.

"Anne is single. I mean, she has an out-of-town boyfriend but I think she's fooling herself. He's been running around on her, you can be sure of that."

"She told you that, when you just met?" I cocked my head curiously.

"She told me enough. Girls know, OK? Anyway, her and some of the other girls are supposed to meet at a club tonight. I might have invited myself along, but I guess you have other plans for Anne." Carolyn winked at me. I shrugged it off.

"I just might." I thought quietly for a minute. "OK, we don't have much to do for a while, and you'll need to entertain yourself tomorrow night. I'm going out."

-10- April 20<sup>th</sup> (Tuesday), Palm Springs, CA

We had a good lazy day. I resisted all urges to go prowling around town or even to scour newspapers for dirt on the Zelatoff company. I had a good plan, and it was best to sit back and let it play out. We had roles to play anyway.

I sent Carolyn out shopping, like any good tourist husband on holiday would. I hoped nobody noticed that she was picking out plain work clothes. I was confident that she would get hired the next day.

She also got us both swimsuits, so I could go play in the pool after all. There were fewer young men in the pool that afternoon. Carolyn was fit into a smartly cut two-piece and sitting up on the deck. She was on her own making up stories to tell the fellows who tried to make conversation with her.

I may have gotten a couple dirty looks when I collected her to leave the pool. If they really thought we were a couple, they might have been sore about this middle-age man keeping a rare young woman to himself.

"When I'm gone, you'll have to tell them I had business in the region. You came along to make it a combination holiday, and I should be back in a few days," I explained as we took turns changing for dinner.

"That's what I already told that captain this afternoon," she called out through the open door of the restroom. "When do you think you'll leave?"

"I'll stick around until I'm sure everything is settled tomorrow; maybe longer, I don't know yet." I dug through my suitcase picking out a suit for the evening. "Say, what do you think of this suit for tonight?"

Carolyn's head and bare shoulder peeked out from behind the vanity area wall. "You said you wanted to look nice, but like you still were working all day, right?" She looked over the matching jacket and pants I was holding up. "Put a lighter shirt with that and I can mess it up for you just enough."

We got dressed and had a small early dinner in the hotel. She had me scrunch up the suit jacket and press it behind me while we ate. Before I left she loosened my tie and put it a little bit askew.

I hadn't had a drink with dinner, but she dipped two fingers into her muddy cocktail and smeared a bit to one side of my collar. "That shouldn't stain, but will leave a dark spot for a bit, and it will smell like you came from somewhere a little shady."

I didn't see a mirror handy, so I trusted her work as it was. "I may get back late, but you be ready for an early start, and wake me up when you're almost ready."

68

With an impish grin she chided me, "Don't you go carousing too hard now. I don't have bail money to come get you out!"

"I'll try to keep it all on the QT, or at least not get caught." I put on my hat and went out into the warm evening.

I saw less than half a dozen cars on the drive west across town. The former resort town was laboring through an overtime workweek, and it was a school night. It was a bit early for night life among those still up for it. I wanted to get a little gas, but the only station I passed was closed.

I considered leaving my car there and walking the last couple blocks to the Chi Chi Club, but I reminded myself that it was more than OK if any Zelatoff people recognized my car that evening. I drove right to the front entrance.

A bored young valet parked my burgundy Lincoln, the one with a sleeker grill than its late model year called for. Inside I talked to the host and told him I was in town on brief business, had been really busy, and was looking to let off a little steam. That prompted a usual spiel for new guests.

The Chi Chi Club was one of only two places on the Palm Springs 'strip' still doing live entertainment on weeknights. It had a pretty high class reputation before the war. He looked me over and he decided I was good enough for their reputation as it was then.

I checked my hat and went looking for the toilet, which was on a hallway between the club and an adjoining hotel. I reviewed my not-overly-nice appearance and went into the club's main room.

The room was too big, the air was too cold, and the lights were too bright. I entered down a few stairs from one corner of the square hall. Two small bars took up part of the walls to the left and right. The left one was shorter by the length of a swinging door to the kitchen. Opposite me was a stage of two tiered white risers, sized for a twenty-piece orchestra behind a dance act.

The live entertainment for that night was a tinny three piece, guitar, horn, and drums, attempting to sound like any radio of the day. They had set up on the second riser and were twenty feet from the nearest empty seats.

The girls from the Zelatoff office were not hard to find. There were three of them together among thirty-some people in the club. My acquaintance Anne was with them. I tried to spy on what she was drinking and maybe send another over. But I decided to take the direct route. I got myself a drink and moved toward a table near them.

"Well how's this for luck?!" I exclaimed after catching a look of recognition in Anne's eye. I stood by their table just to chat for a moment. Anne made introductions which were promptly forgotten. The other girls were appreciably younger than her, maybe teenagers. She was not hard to separate from them.

At another table Anne Baxter and I talked about the weather for as long as one can in the desert. I told her about how busy I was and how much driving around

I had to do. I confided in her about having a 'special' setup for gas rations. The conversation was relaxed and I kept our glasses wet.

She asked just the right questions along the way, seemingly enamored with the idea of an exciting P.I. life, right out of the movies, which is how I was spinning it. When she was out of questions (and I was out of fresh stories), I got to the point.

"I have to be honest with you now," I said as I put out an unfinished cigarette.

"Oh, how's that?" She stopped short of sipping the drink in her hand, brow raised.

"I didn't run into you tonight just by accident. I was hoping to find you."

She set down the drink without it ever getting to her lips. "How did you know... wait, what for??"

"I have a job in mind for you. I'm in a real bind, and after meeting you last week I thought I could trust you to see some important things through."

"Oh, I'm all ears!" The band leader mumbled something over the loudspeakers about the next song as Anne leaned over the table to be heard better. "But I already have a day job, you know."

I leaned in a little myself, not uncrossing my legs. "Ditch it. They'll be here when you get back, if you decide to come back. I can pay you thirty dollars a week, for starters, including a room, and we need someone right away for at least two months."

"Thirty? And who's we?? This is all a bit much, and..."

"I can get you on a bus to Tucson tomorrow morning. Zelatoff will get along fine without you." I pointed a thumb toward the girls with the forgotten names.

"Bus? Oh, I have my own car, so..."

"You do?" I was pulling my wallet out of a jacket pocket. "Great! That's forty a week then, and you can get a few other things done." I handed her a card and four ten dollar bills. "Call this number when you get to Tucson. He'll show you where you'll be staying and brief you on the case."

I had called Professor Arthur earlier and conscripted him into finding ways to keep Miss Baxter busy, and to keep an eye on her. For his trouble he got whatever actual use he could get out of her.

In the morning Carolyn would present herself at Zelatoff again, reminding them of her qualifications as a secretary and lead mail clerk – a position which was suddenly vacant.

## -11- April 21st (Wednesday), Palm Springs, CA

The morning started early. We had to repeat the bus ride routine from Monday, but Carolyn had to be at the Zelatoff office before it opened, which was 7:30 am. We hurried through the practiced routine of sharing the hotel bathroom and got a quick diner breakfast among other townies on their way to regular jobs.

In the car we reviewed the things Carolyn was supposed to look for. "And remember, the single most important thing is to simply do your job well. The whole thing is blown if you lose the job, or don't gain their trust."

"So are you going to lay down some rule like, 'no snooping at all on the first day'?" she asked dryly.

"No. If I was to make a rule, for you it would be, 'no snooping at all for the whole first month'. But I don't see much point in making rules for you."

That got her to smile. "You don't need to worry about me. I'll blend in like a pig in a mud puddle."

"Good, just don't track any mud into my car." She got me to smile now. "You have the number to call me for a pickup?"

"Sure do. But I have no idea how long I could be. I could get a bus back just fine." She waved the dog-eared bus route map.

"Remember that I have a whole lot of nothing to do. Ring up from a pay phone when the first bus lets you off and we'll figure it out." I stopped to let her out in front of a closed store front. Then I set out to make something productive out of the day. This meant a bigger than usual dose of coffee and local newspapers.

The local papers had not picked up the routine of reporting on matters of business and industry. I would find neither news nor speculation about contracts awarded to Zelatoff. Space was given up to mention planned deployments or expansions of the Army air bases, as an introduction to discussions of what it meant to the remaining hospitality industry. Cabanas and cocktails were still the town's bread and butter, as far as the writers knew.

News from the wire services mentioned that it was Adolf Hitler's birthday. A pre-written statement from the Royal Air Force and our Army Air Corps spelled out how many birthday presents they should already have delivered to der Führer that morning.

Entertainment news pivoted on which stars were working hardest to show how hard they were working for the USO and on the last bond drive. The local air base had no shortage of small shows from home town entertainers – which was a phone book of Hollywood A-listers. A story about Bob Hope was dressed up in intrigue. He was due to tour the west coast the next month, and a semi-secret campaign was on to make sure his troupe did a full show in Palm Springs.

I didn't expect to get much from the local library, but out of habit I had to do all my proper footwork. One could read about the history of the area back to the Indian tribes that used to roam it. I could look at photos of what used to be where the Zelatoff factory was. Nothing gave up the most recent history, the few years that saw five city blocks mowed down and the factory erected. Books about it weren't written yet, and the newspapers on hand didn't go back far enough.

My homework was done for the moment. Under high afternoon sun I took off out of town for a drive. It was getting hot, as it had been every day that week. With jacket and tie off I made my own breeze on my way to the mountain pass south of Palm Springs.

The freebie map I had showed the state highway through the mountains as a partial long question mark. A better map showed it more like a chaotic scribble from an angry kindergartener, and the legend claimed it was freshly paved.

There was a vanishingly small possibility of other traffic on the road. I let my car breathe and sweat better than it had in months, tempered only by thoughts of my tires. They were real tires, bought new through a web of deals and favors too layered to remember anymore. If I had to replace them, I probably couldn't. No number of ration coupons, legit or not, could make a set of good rubber doughnuts materialize.

The air cooled as I climbed into the Santa Rosa mountains. Near what I guessed to be the high point of the road, still well under the main ridge line to the east, I stopped to get out and walk around for a few minutes. The desert landscape was seasoned by a salt-and-pepper of the hardy low bushes that cling to life in such places.

I surveyed some of the closer hilltops and thought about what great photos one could get from some of those vantage points, if I waited until sunset, and if I had the camera with me in the first place. Satisfied that the scenery would wait patiently for me to come back another evening, I motored back into town at an easy pace.

In the hotel room I got freshened up, ordered a little food and a pitcher of beer to the room, and called Tucson. Professor Arthur was called to the phone at the gun club office, where he was often welcomed to do business by the range manager.

His new 'employee' was already busy staking out a gas station which had been closed for months. He had plenty of other chores for her, but wanted to get her behind the eight ball with a late night job to start. If she was tired for the whole stint, she was less likely to get ambitious and start asking questions.

"That sounds like a solid plan," I affirmed, "but did you check about getting her on the police payroll for anything?" Paying her straight up cash bait was the most expensive part of this operation so far, enough that it stung a little.

I could hear the professor smirk at my discomfort. "That's a definite maybe. The detective bureau doesn't have anything hot at the moment, but he did admit to being short-staffed, and open to getting help."

"Well I hope they get busy then. Hang on." I let in the room service tray, tipped the young man on the cheap side, and got back to the phone. "I'll check back with you again Friday. You can get me here if something comes up sooner. But don't leave a message, try for me direct."

He understood and we hung up. I ate and drank and fiddled with the radio waiting on Carolyn to call.

## -12- April 23rd (Friday), Palm Springs, CA

Carolyn said her first day was perfectly uneventful. She had to fake her way through knowing some of the latest office machines, but she thought everyone bought her stories and accepted her as just another new girl.

She was keen to share with me what the other girls were keen to share about the recently departed Anne. Anne did have a boyfriend, in Albuquerque. The consensus was that she was indeed being two-timed. In between gossip sessions Carolyn had been doing a lot of mail sorting and filing, which was perfect.

Thursday and Friday we went through the same routine. Carolyn went to work and I tried to stay a little bit busy and a lot amused. I planned to stay in Palm Springs until the weekend to be sure things were working out with her, then head back to Tucson.

I went shopping for better hot weather clothes. I wasn't alone in that department, as it had gotten near 100 degrees several times lately. It was almost too cold in the theater when I sat in my new open weave tweed-like suit jacket through a matinee screening of

Casablanca for the third time. I wondered why some studio movies come out as haphazard jumbles and others of the same budget and supposed tier of talent are tight and focused.

On Friday I spied on the back side of the Zelatoff factory, watching all manner of trucks come and go from the many loading bays. Some of the cleaner newer vehicles had Zelatoff logos on the side. I followed a pair of them far enough to see them get on a northern highway which would route them toward San Francisco.

Other commercial trucks from various lines took other routes, generally due east or west. One single medium-size box van, completely naked of brand markings, went due south. It picked up the same highway on which I'd had a joy ride two days before.

It was almost time to meet Carolyn at the bus so I turned back and tooled by the Zelatoff factory one more time before heading across town. Activity at the loading docks was done for the day. I drove eastward along the length of the building to leave. At the office end I started to speed away then hit my brakes hard, immediately hoping that no one had noticed the gobsmacked P.I. staring at the front door.

Walking out of the office block at just that moment was the deep-faced man, the diminutive passenger of the truck I had lost over a week before. His craggy nose, bony cheeks, and cavernous eye sockets could not be mistaken.

Sometimes people talk about a scientific discovery happening "by luck," but they discount that the discovery happened in the lab of a diligent researcher who had painstakingly set up experimental equipment and who was prepared to observe the result. I had just made my own luck.

I watched the man get into a common brown sedan and moved to where I could see him leave and hopefully follow. I knew that he knew me and my car, so I would have to lay back, but I desperately wanted to see where he went.

I checked my watch. Carolyn would have to get back on her own.

My target turned out and headed east. I tried to keep a couple cars between us as I followed. It wasn't easy, as few private cars were out in that early evening. A mile from the factory I swerved out from behind an Army truck and ran straight through a red light to keep the other sedan in sight.

Short city blocks clicked by anonymously. Tacky tourist shops and shuttered luxury car dealers offered no distraction for me right then.

Another mile down the same road he pulled sharply into a small motel parking lot. I cut to the side of the street and stopped, hopefully quicker than the man could turn to look behind him for an erratically behaving tail car. After a pause I again moved at a normal pace toward the motel.

All room doors of the motel were exposed to the street. My acquaintance had not stopped at the motel office. He was parked in front of one of the rooms and was getting a small case from the trunk of his car. I drove by and circled the block to make another pass. He was inside when I drove by the second time.

I checked my watch again. I figured the guy would be in the room for at least a little while. I took off at some speed to cover another mile to the south. I met Carolyn just as she got off her second bus. She pretended not to notice me as she passed my car. I pulled out and spun the car around to race ahead of her again, stopped and sounded the horn repeatedly as I waved her in.

She got in quickly, and I had the car moving again before her door was closed. "I suppose we're in a rush now. What's up?" she asked matter-of-factly.

"We need to watch somebody. With any luck we'll get to tail him somewhere." I was focused on driving but glanced over to see her sit up and smile at the news of more exciting work. We hustled back toward the little motel, slowing to drive past again. The deep-faced man's car was still there.

Sunset was getting near. I parked at the end of the next side street a bit west of the motel. From there I could watch without being blinded by the sun. We waited while I explained to Carolyn just who we were watching.

As I wrapped up the very short story as it was, she reached into her purse. "Since, we're waiting, here is what I have so far." She held up a thin book-size notepad with a printed cardboard cover bearing the Zelatoff logo.

"Already? Didn't we agree no spying on the first week?" I asked as she handed me the pad. The first sheet had about a dozen company names and addresses on it with a few shorthand notes next to each. By touch I could tell many more pages behind it had been written on.

"Actually it was going to be the whole first month, but we compromised and I gave it a whole day." She looked at my face for a reaction, but didn't seem too concerned about whether it was good or bad. "Let me show you what's what."

Carolyn pointed out the details of each entry. Each was an address to which some company correspondence had come or gone. If she knew what was in it, the extra marks denoted if it was an invoice, a payment, or a letter, and what kind of thing was being traded.

She had to write all this down surreptitiously, and only got data on about two in ten pieces that she handled. This gave us over a hundred names and addresses.

I was completely unprepared for a stakeout. We had no provisions, and I hadn't put us near any restroom to use. Carolyn didn't say a word about needing dinner or anything else. She understood the situation.

We sat almost two hours before anything happened. I couldn't see our target's motel room from our parking spot, but I could see the tail end of his car and the motel office. By dim streetlight the man appeared at the car, putting his small suitcase in the trunk. He went to the motel office for a moment then back to his car.

I got my own car started and into gear. I backed up a little farther out of sight. The man's dark sedan, a different dull brown in the street lights, moved past us casually. I waited a slow four count then pulled out behind him.

He turned south, driving the whole way past the Army air field. This helped me by providing a few military vehicles for cover between me and my prey. When that road ended he bore left again, taking the state highway along the dark side of the mountain ridge that defined Palm Springs. Traffic thinned out and I had fewer other cars for cover.

I hung back as far as I dared without losing the other car. If he turned suddenly I would have to charge forward and get a look down the side street as quick as I could. He kept an easy pace all the way out of town past the little cottage resorts and quiet golf course hotels. He made a lazy southerly turn onto another state highway, the same road I'd taken up into the mountains twice in the last week.

If you ever read about a gumshoe who can follow anybody anywhere, solo, and not be noticed doing it, forget about it. It's not possible. Facing us was an unbroken forty-mile-long stretch of two lane road with essentially zero traffic on it. One car cannot follow another that whole way and not register with the other driver. It's dead easy for the lead driver, if he's at all suspicious, to burn a tail just by pulling over anywhere. The chase driver has to either give up the plot or blow on by casually and be sure never to be seen in that car again.

There are some things one can do to even the odds though, and I had a few of them working for me. It was night, so my car color and model wouldn't register at a distance. A great trick I could work at night was with the extra headlamps I had installed. They were smaller bulbs, set behind the grill inside and lower than the main lights. From a distance they looked like a different model car, one further back than it really was. A pair of switches to the left of my steering wheel would switch between the sets of lights, or kill the right headlight to mimic yet a different, and more poorly maintained, vehicle.

I had another reason to be glad Carolyn was with me. A couple looks less suspicious, and to change our look again I could let her drive solo for a shift while I hid in the back seat area. (Like I said there was no back seat, but there was still a sizable storage space between the extra fuel tanks.)

The deep-faced man accelerated on the climb out of town. He had no love of speed limits on this night. Having driven much of the road already I knew there was nowhere for him to turn for a long way, so I gave him a long leash. I came out of turns just catching glimpses of his taillights.

He knew the winding road, better than me. Even with a mundane car he made me work the controls well to keep up. I kept my regular headlights on, as it would be odd for the car behind him to change anywhere on the singular road.

Carolyn kept an eye on the map by flashlight. It showed little useful detail except approximate intersections of the few state highways. At the first dark crossroads town, which was barely a mule stop, our mark turned down a dirt road to the southwest. I drove past the turn, cut back to the intersection, and resumed following with the different headlights on. The road was dry and following his dust trail was easy, if seeing the road was not.

For another hour and a half the pattern was repeated as our rabbit zig-zagged through the valleys that divide the many mountain clusters of southernmost California. I closed distance as we finally came into the first town of any substance, on a saddle-shaped plateau where two canyon roads met two passes up into neighboring mountain ranges.

The target car turned down the main drag of the town and cruised through to the far end. One could see the lights of a late night service station from miles away under the star lit sky. I anticipated the other car pulling in and it did, to the right. I turned left down a side street just short of the station, circling the block with my lights out. The station was the only one I'd seen for hours, probably the only one in the county. The regional gasoline board could hardly put its share of gasoline anywhere else to be sold.

We spied from the shadows across the street as the man stopped by one of the gas pumps, lit from two sides by bright lights on the service station's small building. He tended to his vehicle then went inside the building. I expected he would be inside a few minutes and moved to take advantage. I hustled my car across the street to a spot beside the building, out of its lights.

I grabbed a trusty old hunting knife from the glove box. I motioned for Carolyn to get out quietly and wait behind the car. "My camera is in the trunk. Try to get a picture of this guy, without him noticing. I'm going to try something. When he comes out of the building, close the trunk, hard so I can hear it."

She had the camera case open in a blink. "Is it a focal plane shutter?"

I hesitated to answer, "Um, yeah. I mean, I think so." She was looking up at the available lights. She made adjustments to the camera as I snuck around the outside of the station's front lot, to come up on the shadowed side of the deep faced man's car.

I got to the car and went for the rear tire on that side, feeling the side and tread of it. If this fellow was in the habit of crossing over western states very often, he would need to get tires wherever he could. This one was a cheap retread, with an obvious seam where the overmold was mismatched to the core. The tread felt firm, but slimy, almost tacky. This suited me just fine. It was badly cured and would cut easily.

I worked hurriedly with the knife, bearing down on the pommel and pushing on the back side of the blade until it hurt. I worked it into an angled cut across the lousy tread rubber, as deep as I could manage until I heard my car's trunk lid slam shut.

I peeked up through windows of the sedan to see the deep-faced man looking into the shadows toward the noise. As I snuck back away from the car to find cover behind a shrub, I also heard the soft click of my own camera's shutter.

I wondered what the gas station's landscaping might look like in the day light while waiting for the man to get in his car and disappear down the highway. I strolled casually back to my car. Carolyn already had the camera packed up and was waiting by her open car door to get back in and continue the chase. "Relax, we've got some time," I said to her curious face.

"How's that? Don't we need to see where he goes?" She clutched to the top of the door frame with both hands.

I explained that our prey would likely be cursing the cheap retreads he got stuck with in a few dozen miles. "So we get a break here. You can use the facilities first." She practically skipped to the front door of the station.

I followed inside and met the young station attendant. He didn't know anything about the deep-faced man except he'd been in a time or two before. He reminded me that it was almost eleven o'clock and he needed to close up. I bought a couple Cokes and snacks from a rack behind him, handing them to Carolyn on her way out so I could also use the restroom.

We got moving again and I asked Carolyn to get out her notes from Zelatoff. "We'll be near San Diego in a couple more hours. We pushed our luck following that guy this far. I want to get ahead of him, and we'll just have to guess at where we need to go. So start flipping through that pad and pick out any San Diego addresses."

"Do you really think we'll find it like that?" She was already scanning her notes but was not convinced about the utility of the exercise.

"I don't even know what 'it' is. But our guy has done us the favor of narrowing it down to one corner of the country." For a few minutes there was only the sound of page turning and writing until I exclaimed, "Shoot! Don't you have to work tomorrow?"

"Actually no. Only some of the office staff work on Saturdays, and none this weekend."

"Oh, that's lucky." I was glad to have that settled.

Carolyn had stopped transcribing. "Because of Sunday," she added. She watched for some sign of the connection being made.

"Sunday," I repeated. "Holy... It's Easter Sunday isn't it?"

"Not much gets by you, Sherlock." She was back to reading her notes.

It took me another minute to think to ask, "Did you have plans? Do you need to get back to the kids?"

Carolyn didn't stop writing. "It would be nice. At least I need to call back to Tucson and see if someone can be put out to see them dressed and in church."

I thought about it less than a second. "It's going to be a busy day, but we'll get back to Tucson before Sunday morning." I spent the rest of the drive figuring out how that was going to happen.

## -13- April 24<sup>th</sup> (Saturday), San Diego, CA

Neither one of us had ever been to San Diego. Carolyn had found five addresses in her notes that were in San Diego or a nearby town either of us recognized. I drove us through the eastern foothills to the southern end of the city so we could come up the harbor side and end in downtown.

We only had a sidebar map of major roads around the city. I didn't want to be on major roads that late at night in a coastal city full of war plants and Navy docks. I tried to stay a couple blocks in from the harbor and industrial strip that hugged it. The city grids mostly obliged.

In due time we got to where I thought was near the first address on our list. Next to the entry for Rohr Aerostructures Carolyn had noted, "Invoice, 'Covers, aluminum, formed'." It was probably legit, in fact all the places on our list probably had legitimate business with Zelatoff, but these were the leads we had.

Very few streetlights were lit on the inland roads, and none on the bay front highway. I turned my car across lanes several times to lay its headlights on dark street signs.

Traffic was nonexistent. Some parking lots were full to the brim with cars, outside blacked-out buildings throbbing with third shift production. I had my window down, taking in the cooler sea side air. Carolyn might have been cold in her desert work dress, but she didn't complain.

Pairs of men could be made out standing in the dark at some intersections. One of them shone a powerful flashlight into my car as we rolled by.

Finally we hit some traffic. My headlights revealed a Navy shore patrol uniform on a young man who stopped us. He was letting cars out of a lot belonging to a tall silhouette of a building that stretched out into the dark ocean. It was Rohr Aerostructures, letting out a shift.

I was startled by a knock on the rear quarter window behind me. Another Navy MP, as young as the one directing traffic, had come up behind us.

"Good evening." He didn't wait to exchange greetings. "What's the idea of coming down here with your lights on full like that?" The cars leaving the plant all had headlights of low power installed, or had their lenses taped over to leave narrow slits, admitting barely enough light to walk by. The lamps I had installed were extra-bright, probably not strictly legal even before coastal blackout rules.

I tried to sound contrite. "Oh, sorry, sir. I was just in town on business, didn't think to modify the car.

Actually, I didn't expect to be out at night like this at all." For effect I glanced over at Carolyn. The young seaman was already looking at her, sizing up the situation as he looked back at me.

"Say," I continued, "I see everybody leaving but nobody going in. Are they off for the weekend?"

"Nah. This place only works two shifts a day anyway, not like the other factories we look after." He gestured in a wide arc at most of the city inland from us. His face was starkly cross-lit by car headlights from his left. Then he remembered that he was working security, "But who are you asking questions about schedules? Just what kind of work are you doing here anyway?"

I looked back at Carolyn then right at the sailor's face as I pointed toward the rear of the car. He backed up so I could get out. I took him back past the rear wheel and spoke in hushed tones. "Look, it's been a long week. A small company like mine can't even get in the door with these big guys. I took a Friday night out to improve my mood, met this dish, and kinda took up with her. Now I really gotta get her home before her mother gets worried, and in a way so my wife doesn't get worried, either. You follow?"

I had fished out my wallet and was palming a few bills in case the guy needed more convincing. He showed me a tight smile and shook his head. "Alright then, brother. You take good care of the lady. And keep those lights off when you can, OK?"

I shook his hand, put my wallet away, and got back in the car. We followed the last of the Rohr workers up the highway. Carolyn asked, "I did my best 'sit here and look pretty'. Did it work?"

"It worked perfect," I affirmed.

She stared ahead impassively. "When they're young and male it usually does." She became more animated as she looked at me to ask, "So, what did we learn?"

"Rohr is not particularly busy. They might not be a normal fit as a Zelatoff supplier, but they have capacity to spare compared to others, so they'd take any business. If they're supplying aluminum covers, it could be for airplane radios or some such."

Nothing much happened at our next stop, mostly because I couldn't find it. The streets of National City are not winding or complicated. I just didn't know any of them by name. A visit to Western Express Freight would have to wait until daylight when we could get directions or buy a local map. The same would go for Universal Spline & Coupler wherever it was in San Diego. But a pricey sounding law firm promised to be on the downtown grid, so we went there.

A dark granite building face admitted to housing the offices of Fischer, Metzler, and Wislavic behind it. I wondered why Zelatoff would need a lawyer in San Diego, being based elsewhere entirely. Still, it looked like a sizable firm which could recruit clients far afield.

My watch pointed at three o'clock. I found us a quiet alley near a quiet neighborhood to park the car. I remembered an old overcoat in the trunk and offered it to Carolyn as the night air got colder. I closed up my summer weight suit the best I could and sat back for an attempt at sleep.

At first light I saw Carolyn was sleeping comfortably. I let her stay that way for another 30 minutes before I started the cold car and got us moving again.

The city was busy, with a more even mix of vehicles that I'd seen in any war city. Thousands of people were heading in to a Saturday shift; almost as many were heading home from late night labors. Army and Navy vehicles dotted the flow with green and white splotches. The impending holiday may have cut into military traffic more than civilian industry.

The first diner we found open had clean restrooms, a few fresh eggs, and no idea where Universal Spline & Coupler was. But a greasy map on the wall pointed us to a street on the north end of the bay, near the big commercial docks.

We approached the district from the north. The formal San Diego business district gave way to a colorfully shaded assortment of blue collar bars and small service companies. A welding supply company was next to a rigging equipment retailer next to an electric motor repair shop. Busy pier cranes grew up out of the horizon as we approached the harbor.

We turned left down the street where Universal was supposed to be. One block along our way Carolyn grabbed my arm, "There he is!"

"Keep watching," I told her as I casually turned left again up the next side street. "OK, what did you see?"

94

"That was his car. I remember the license number, a New Mexico plate." I had failed to notice the car I had been following for hours just two blocks ahead of us. And through hours of tailing I had never thought to take down the deep-faced man's plate number. I paused for a moment, more wondering if I was getting too old than deciding what to do next. What to do was the easy part.

"OK, you get out and walk down that block. I'll meet you on the next cross street." I gave her a few more detailed instructions and sent her off.

I drove slowly around the block, giving Carolyn time to get to the car. It was parked in front of a row of old two-story masonry buildings, facing more of the same. The individual addresses had been every variety of shop or bar or garage over their years. At that time most were closed up, windows boarded or painted over. Government contracts were going to the big guys first – there was no time to build up a supply base of smaller shops. Universal Spline & Coupler had no immediate neighbors.

I paused before the next intersection to watch Carolyn approach the car. On cue she 'dropped' something near the front of the dark sedan. She steadied herself with a hand on its hood as she bent down to retrieve her lost item. While straightening her dress she ambled closer to the front of the building. It had a tall bay door next to a man door and painted-over window front. Carolyn eyed all three closely as she continued moving down the sidewalk. I rolled through the intersection to meet her around the corner.

She got in and reported without any prompting. "The engine is still warm. The paint is scratched up around the wheel where you cut the tire; it must have whipped around a bunch before coming off entirely. The roll-up door is newer than the last paint job on the building." She told me this and was looking at me ready to hear what came next. She wasn't waiting for my approval to confirm that she'd done a good job.

I wanted to get inside that building. We could wait until night to break in, but I didn't have any tools and there was no guarantee the deep-faced man was leaving any time soon. I kept going around the block again to look behind the old garage front that housed Universal. The other side of the block was a different row of sparsely occupied shop spaces. A narrow alley, barely walkable, separated the rows.

I got us back onto the street where the deep-faced man's car was parked and put us a couple hundred feet away to the west, parked behind a post box that would block a clean view of my car. We watched for a while. I admitted to Carolyn that I didn't know what we were looking for, which she accepted with a knowing nod.

Two hours passed. I was ready to call a lunch break and plan to come back later when we came into more made luck. Another vehicle, an older Ford panel van, pulled up in front of Universal. We were too far away to make out its California plate. The small truck parked on the street and two men got out, both in plain suits. One of them tapped on the opaque glass of the shop until the man door next to it opened.

I had my camera ready, with the longer lens on it. The obstructions I had put between us didn't allow many good shots, but I kept clicking.

The deep-faced man came out, closing the door behind him. He spoke to the new pair animatedly, pointing at his car and gesturing around where the tire had come unraveled on him some hours before. At the close of the conversation both new men shook their heads slowly as their companion shrugged with both open palms in the air.

He opened the trunk of his car and the taller of the other pair reached in to haul out a car wheel with the shredded remnants of a tire carcass clinging to it. The Universal Spline & Coupler bay door was opened and the deep-faced man drove his car inside. The mid-day San Diego air was pleasant and they left the door open.

"I have an idea," said Carolyn.

"You have an idea about how we're going to get inside?" I had both hands on the steering wheel, waiting for any excuse to move them into more productive action.

"I have an idea for how *I* am going to walk right in there," she turned to me with an eager smile. "But, it means we have to go shopping again." She grinned at me as she dreamed up a shopping list.

A flurry of asking and following directions got us in and out of a downtown clothing shop, a ladies' accessory boutique, and a neighborhood bakery. The bakery was happy to lend Carolyn a couple of their big trays to carry everything, especially after she insisted on taking all their less consistent products, misshapen pieces that could have come out of an inexperienced young housewife's kitchen.

With Carolyn suitably attired and equipped, including a small notepad for a receipt book, I let her out to sell baked goods for her supposed pet charity. The line was that she was raising money for child care centers for workers at the smaller war plants, places too small to have their own facilities. Her group was hitting up all the local small businesses around San Diego for contributions.

We started two blocks up from Universal, after checking that the men's cars were still on the street. Not many places were open and occupied, but Carolyn must have talked a good game. Her new dress was just barely appropriate for someone's wife to be walking around an industrial district. We made almost ten bucks before she got to the block with Universal on it.

It was an excruciating wait. I sat parked around the corner, in the same spot where I had waited for her before. Ten minutes passed, then fifteen. I was debating if twenty or thirty minutes would be my cue to barge in on the party, when Carolyn passed through my rear view mirror. I pulled around to meet her at the next street. Her newly empty tray went in the trunk and she got in.

I pulled away smoothly. I turned to ask jokingly if we should find a spot to sell the other tray of sweets. Carolyn was curled up in her seat, face in her hands, visibly shaking.

I let her work through it for a while, driving nowhere quietly. Finally I asked, "When did it all set in?"

She was composed enough by then to lean back in her seat, head back, staring at the roof. "Not 'til I was almost back in the car. I thought about everything, all at once, all the things that could have gone wrong." After a pause she sat up straight and looked at me. "Oh, Nick, those are awful men, violent men. I think they would kill you for a pack of gum."

"For you I'm sure they would ask two packs," I reassured her. She didn't think it was funny. I expounded, "That's the way it goes. Before the act it's all according to plan. You think of what you can think of, and on some level you're ready for all that. Only later do the nerves really get rattled, when you think of everything else that could have happened.

"Beforehand, it's just common stage fright, nothing more. But an actor on stage never got done then thought about every chance every person in the audience had to shoot him for missing a line."

I circled around downtown San Diego while she made her report. Just the three men we saw were inside Universal. It was all one open room, two stories high. Inside the tall bay door was a new electric crane. In the back of the room were exactly two pieces of heavy equipment. A new machinist's lathe was set up but not connected to power, and it still had shipping wax all over it. Another piece next to it was still inside a ten-foot-long crate. Carolyn's initial note with the Universal

Spline & Coupler address had listed 'machining services' from the mailed invoice. No metal was being cut there.

To the left were many work benches, some with electrical tools on them. It was the only area showing signs of recent activity. The men had been working there and it was an area they seemed keen to steer Carolyn away from. There were two telephones on the middle bench, side-by-side, one with a normal dial the other with only three push buttons across where a dial should be.

"They acted nice enough, but they got up and moved around me. I was being herded like by sheep dogs, or more like wolves. One of them picked up a long pipe and went behind me to look outside. They were ready to buy me out though, to get rid of me I guess. I took my time showing them each item while I peeked around them."

"They kept pressing me back toward the open door. Finally, I had my heels on the sidewalk so I took their money and left. They said 'keep the change' and dropped the door right behind me." She brought out a twenty-dollar bill and handed it to me. I held it for a moment, tempted to hand it back with a, 'that's your first bonus.' I thought better of it and pocketed the bill.

"Oh and there were two cots in back, and a lot of big batteries," she added

"You mean like for a lantern?" I asked.

"No, no, the big kind. In satchels, like for army radios. There were shelves full of them in the far corner from the door."

I didn't have any immediate theory for that. I doubled back to the biggest news stand we had passed and got the day's local newspapers. The owner let me pick through his returns for old business sections, which saved me a whole dollar.

I burned up much more than that in gas to hustle through the mountains winding our way east. We made it back to Tucson just after sunset. I counted out another week's pay to Carolyn (I would need to visit the bank again soon) and left her at her apartment.

-14- April 25<sup>th</sup> (Easter Sunday), Tucson, AZ

Sunday morning, Easter Sunday, I fed myself out of the meager pantry in my little house. I didn't expect much to be open in town. I needed to hit the library again, find a photo lab, and get some letters mailed.

All that would have to wait another day. I started a couple of the letters, but I would have to see the photos before I finished them. My day would be spent buried in old newspapers again, those from San Diego.

I indulged myself in reading much of the local news and human interest pieces. "A Day in the Life of a Coastal Battery Gunner" was a sappy piece about a young sailor named David, probably fictional, stuck on land, living out a bleak existence staring at the ocean. He longed for home as much any guy stuck on Guadalcanal, and was doing his part to protect America, but wouldn't get the glory of being in the fight. Too bad for little Davey.

A more serious companion column documented some of the reported Japanese submarine sightings off the San Diego shore line. Those too were probably all fictional, and the military wasn't confirming anything. But the couple Jap boats that really did lob shells at California in the previous few months would keep a lot of Californians staring at the water for a long time. One military man interviewed lamented the distraction from false alarms, while appreciating that the population was showing some vigilance.

I gave my morning over to the news. Big and small, world-shaking and trivial, none of it mattered to me. I read it anyway. It was something of a break, reading about road paving projects in Riverside County, or bridge demolition jobs in Africa.

I started a third pot of coffee before getting into my real work for the day. I had twenty business sections from two different publishers, going back over two weeks.

The law firm Fischer, Metzler, and Wislavic was mentioned often. It had its hands in lot of different practices, no surprise. Most often it represented a client in suits over business matters. Some were inter-company, but they seemed to specialize in representing companies against the United States government, especially its War Department – the leading buyer of just about everything.

I worked through the news by date, oldest to newest. Government contracts that weren't secret were listed in regular tables. Those that were secret were given away by plant expansions or desperate ads for experienced foremen (which might as well have been asking for Martians).

Ads and free reminders to buy war bonds were ubiquitous. The papers should simply have been printed on war bond posters. I thought about buying another $25 certificate at the post office the next day. I decided it would depend on what my banker said in the morning.

No mention came up of Universal Spline & Coupler, which was expected. I didn't think I'd find them in the business directories at the library either (but I was still going to look when it opened). The very last fold of newspaper I handled was an afternoon run from the day before. The obituaries had been shuffled into that Saturday's business section by the editors. A small picture there caught my eye.

The driver of the truck, the original red-cabbed flatbed that I had lost, was dead. Samuel Windham, aged 52, widower, remaining family in Sacramento, had been working as a professional driver only a few years. He had been a general tradesman of sorts around Sacramento before that.

The obituary mentioned suspicious circumstances and pointed me toward news about the case. I tore back through the pile of trash-heap-bound papers. A Friday afternoon printing had a short mention. More detail was found in a Saturday morning piece.

> Yesterday morning a San Diego resident was killed when his vehicle plunged off the side of US-80 in the In-Ko-Pah Mountains pass, police reports say. Circumstances are suspicious.

Samuel Windham was driving his own car, a 1938 Plymouth sedan, which exited the road at speed just short of a guard rail. The car entered a deep ravine. It would have fallen a great distance and sustained inestimable damage except that it struck squarely a recently installed utility pole. Mr. Windham is believed to have died shortly after this impact.

The police report notes clear weather and good road conditions. No witnesses are known to have seen the incident.

An official police statement says that an investigation is open and anyone with information about Mr. Windham's recent whereabouts or business contacts is invited to be interviewed. A confidential source close to the case says Mr. Windham's car was tampered with, in a way which would make the brakes ineffective.

I checked my watch. There were still a dozen hours left until Monday morning business hours. I was now desperately anxious to get things moving. I needed more information, and I needed other people to get it for me.

It was time to meet Carolyn again. I drove across Tucson to a prearranged location near her apartment. I parked on the street and got out to join her staring into the window of a soda shop that was closed, as if we each had hoped it to be open and were disappointed by the holiday closing sign.

She carried a comfortable glow with her, refreshed by a short day with her little family. I got right to business, explaining about the newly dead man and some of the things I had to get done next.

Carolyn would take the earliest bus back to Palm Springs to return to work at Zelatoff. I considered driving her back and continuing into San Diego, but my hours were better spent on the phone and mailing letters, multiplying the number of people working on my problem.

Also I seriously had to think about when I might next be able to get tires for the Lincoln. I didn't have an honest lead on rationed rubber yet. A dishonest lead wasn't coming up either.

## -15- April 26th (Monday), Tucson AZ

I didn't set an alarm. I was up before six. By five minutes after eight I was showered, dressed, fed, and standing outside a photo lab sipping coffee from a paper cup.

The lab hadn't opened yet. I picked it because I thought it was a good professional shop, being attached to a high-end camera retailer and servicer. The weather was perfect – clear, dry and comfortable. Across the flat suburban landscape the ever present mountain backdrop was unusually detailed.

The shop door was opened from the inside and I was hot on the heels of its owner. I presented my film and told him what I needed. He agreed to an early afternoon pickup. I left and headed toward the university.

Parking near the university's main library was no trouble that early on a weekday. In fact, the library didn't open until nine. Its outer lobby was unlocked though so I made use of a bank of pay phones there. I left a message at the gun club, confident that Professor Arthur would get it that morning.

That chore took little time. I made myself sit down outside and relax for a few minutes. Over a slow cigarette I wondered about the names of the birds that I only then noticed flitting and hopping about the neat courtyard. I wondered about the names of the trees that someone had chosen for landscaping outside the University of Arizona library.

When she unlocked the library I didn't chase the librarian as closely as I had the photo lab owner. In good time I was directed to a corner of the reference section with business directories and to a stack of out-of-town phone books.

As expected, I found prominent listings for the Fischer, Metzler, and Wislavic law firm, the kind you have to pay extra for. Also as expected, I found not even the most minimal announcement of Universal Spline & Coupler. I looked up a couple other law firms, ones I had written down from San Diego newspaper ads.

Moving on to the San Diego phone books, I checked the same names, looking over yellow pages ads if a company had one. I also looked at listed private investigators. I made a short list of them based on not much more than the small print names.

I still had time before my lunch appointment, so I made some change at the library front desk and went back to the pay phones. A long bank of open phones was terminated by a pair of private wood-sided booths. I picked one of the San Diego law offices from my list and got connected to it.

A young lady at the Kramer & Hodges firm answered and transferred me to an even younger sounding junior attorney. The firm's ad highlighted specialization in family law. I knew this sometimes meant some heavy records searching, such as for Baby Doe adoption cases, and I expected they could handle my job easily.

Any title company or research service, or even another P.I., could have done the work, for less money. But a real lawyer can be reasonably expected to maintain confidentiality.

I described what I needed, promising to send a formal letter with the exact details. "Very well," the attorney said. "We will start as soon as we get your letter, along with some verification of your identity. Just a routine requirement, you understand."

I hadn't thought hiring a lawyer hundreds of miles away would be perfectly simple. "Would a check drawn on a Tucson bank be sufficient verification?"

"Uh, yes. Yes, certainly, that will do." The young man was adding up billable hours in his head so loud I could hear it.

"I thought so." I reminded him that it was a rush job, accepted his quoted rate with a grimace, and hung up. I had about forty minutes left to make lunch.

I made a couple stops for gasoline, taking four or five gallons at a time. I didn't like ever letting my tanks get as low as they were. I also didn't like getting dirty looks when I took on twice as much as most families were allowed in a whole week. As it was I would have to keep track of where I'd filled up so as not to show up too soon after, raising questions about my business.

At the third place I was helped by a familiar face. "Here, let me get that for ya, Nick!" said the attendant as he snatched up the fuel hose just ahead of me. It was Mike Minervini, from New Jersey. I had last seen him just under a year before, when I was working out who had hijacked an armored car (the easy part) and how they were laundering the cash and bonds it held (the hard part). Everybody called him Smithy, and I never found out why. I never cared either; that was what he was called and that was that.

Smithy was one of those guys who never seems to rise very far, but is awfully well connected from the bottom. He worked sometimes as a mechanic, sometimes as anything else. He may have been a utility guy for some mobsters, or he may have just hung out in the same places as their actual henchmen. All I knew was he could be counted on to get information when I needed it.

"Smithy, you're like a little dog, always under foot." I mused for a moment at the coincidence of running into him in Arizona. "So just what brings you all the way out here?"

He looked at me sideways with a dumb grin. "A bus!" he deadpanned. "How about you?"

I shook my head again, "All right then, I'll just suppose it was for the weather. Unless... you didn't find out you had a kid back east, did you?"

Smithy stood up straight, letting go of the filler neck. "Hey now, don't even joke like that!" He was smiling at the needling though. "OK, truth is, the weather is good, plus I got a good job here." He angled a thumb back toward the service station. "The fellow who built this place brought his money from back east. I got asked to come out. The guy was looking for good help and another guy said I'd be good to bring out to work the place."

I looked over the building while Smithy finished writing up my receipt. It was a big new service station, on the north side of a busy street, with four mechanic's bays facing south. It probably did good service business before the war, when they could get both parts and customers. Two of the bays were busy that morning. A taller section of the building continued deep into the lot, continuing the west wall at a right angle to the front section, at least as big as the service area.

I looked closely at Smithy's hand when he passed me back the ration book and receipt, confirming something I'd seen earlier. A blue stain was set into the cuticles and some creases of the skin. I left with a friendly smile, taking one last look at the northern portion of the building.

I ditched my jacket and tie as I crossed under the main highway back to the east side of Tucson. They joined my hat on the rear seat shelf. The noon sun bore down without discrimination on the dirt lots and red tile roofs and sheet steel buildings all around me. A six-wheeled Army truck passed me, seven or eight bored soldiers standing up in the back to get into the artificial breeze.

I was late, on purpose. I had told Professor Arthur to meet me at the El Conquistador for lunch, and to bring Anne Baxter with him. She didn't need to know what I had been up to, just that I was still very busy.

For a change of pace I went into the El Con from the front, through the main lobby. I recognized one of the managers sitting in an overly plush chair trying to settle something with two older Army officers who were sunk into a dainty settee across a low table. None of them looked very happy about whatever the matter was.

I made my way around the reception area and down the glass-covered corridor outside the hotel ballrooms. I came through the formal dining room and into the rear lobby, facing the main pool. A sign by the outside door said "POOL CLOSED FOR SERVICE". Out of curiosity I peeked outside.

Judging by the two broken glass top tables and debris around the pool deck I guessed a very small tornado had touched down. That or a rowdy party of soldiers had met a rowdy party of airmen. The bar host confirmed that the latter theory was correct. He showed me to where he'd sat Anne Baxter and Arthur Mason twenty minutes earlier. An empty water glass and a half finished beer sat between them, respectively.

I shook Professor Arthur's hand then stuck my arm out to Anne. She reached up uncertainly and shook my hand weakly.

"Mister Guyon... are we supposed to know each other? I mean, here, in public," she asked as I sat down.

"Around here, anyone that knows me knows that I know everyone," I boasted with a flourish. "And they know that a friend of Arthur is a friend of mine." I flipped open the menu that had been waiting for me. "You can think of this particular place as home field."

Professor Arthur jumped in before the conversation could develop any further. "Anne has really been on the ball, and she found what just might be the break we were after."

"Well, that might be very good news!" I smiled at Anne and back at the professor. "So, catch me up on what we've learned since you and I last talked." I fixed on Professor Arthur for any clues I was supposed to pick up as he explained.

"You remember that old garage on the south edge of town you wanted looked at, because you thought it was suspicious?" I nodded as if I did remember. "Well, Anne was staking it out for us, until very late at night. Just like you thought, on the second night they showed up."

I nodded again, knowing who 'they' were supposed to be. "How many this time?" I asked him.

"Three," Anne interjected, "three men. They came up in a small van and unloaded at least two dozen cardboard boxes. This was just after midnight."

"It's been vacant for several years now," the professor took back over. "I pulled the business registration records. The owner skipped town facing bankruptcy; he may have had gambling debts, too. No telling who has the keys to the place now. Unless you already know..." He left the stage open for me.

I thought about pretending to think about it for a moment. "I might have an idea, but can't be sure yet." I thought for real another moment. "I need more information, and soon. Anne, I need you to do something tomorrow, after watching the garage again, of course."

She sat up straighter, braced with importance again. "Sure. I'll get it done." We paused as Anne's glass was refilled and we put in food orders.

My beer came as I explained. "I have a lot to get done today still, including a bunch of letters to get out. One of them is real rush now, based on what you discovered, and it needs to be delivered to San Diego." She was up for the job but wondered aloud about gasoline for the trip. I said not to worry and procured a fresh blank A-series ration book from my jacket pocket.

"You do have an 'A' window sticker, right?" She said yes. "Fill in the front like usual for your car type. The book is yours to keep. Just please don't use it in Texas – I'm pretty sure that's where the serial number is from." We went over details of what had to be delivered to where and the best way to get it there. I reassured her about the lack of traffic cops looking for speeders outside of the cities.

"Tomorrow morning, meet me at seven a.m. on Sentinel Peak, at the overlook above the big 'A'. I will give you a sealed envelope for the lawyer. When you get back, meet Arthur at the same spot at nine p.m. to verify that everything went OK."

Anne nodded through all this, repeating key details just to reinforce them in her memory. She excused herself to use the restroom shortly after I finished.

As soon as she was out of earshot Professor Arthur started in on me. "What if I had plans for tomorrow night?" he protested.

"Can it. You're loving this little play." He grinned back at me and admitted so. "What's the deal? You sent her off on a fool's errand and she actually broke a case, is that right?"

"It looks that way," he said with a shrug. We paused as the first plates of food came out. "I had her run a few errands for me then go sit across from some old dump all night. I even showed her how to set herself up right and not been seen. Wouldn't you know it, somebody is running something through the place."

"There's enough of it going around, we shouldn't be surprised," I said while poking at a few undersized steamed vegetables. "It sounds like a cooling off spot, or a firewall."

He nodded, "She says all the boxes were new and the same size. I don't think it's stolen goods. I'd guess counterfeiters. They want to keep stock away from the production location, so the whole operation doesn't get burned at once."

"Firewall then. OK, if it keeps Anne busy, that's fine. Any reason you would need to tell the police?" I had to remind myself that Professor Arthur had been a part-time cop for a long time.

"I'm in no hurry to complicate my life. You're doing just fine at it without my help!" He pointed a fork at me accusingly.

"I appreciate the compliment," I replied before I bit into a fairly good burger with generous trimmings. "Say, this garage," I got out through a busy mouth, "was it a big 'L'-shape with four bays out front?"

"No, just a little place with two doors and no gas pumps. Why?"

"Just checking. Ran into an old scoundrel today at a different place. Maybe we'll watch that one next."

He looked toward where Anne had disappeared before asking, "This letter you've got going to the lawyer, what's it about?" I explained that it asked the lawyer to dig up every public and not-quite-public record on Zelatoff and Universal. "Don't you think she'll peek? Would she report back to someone at Zelatoff?"

"I expect that she will, on both counts. I hope she won't squawk to someone until she can do it at Zelatoff

116

in person, which is looking like next week – I made sure she doesn't have time for the detour tomorrow – but I can't control it if she tries to phone in sooner."

Professor Arthur was gleeful with curiosity at the new wrinkle in the script. "Are you going to fill me in on this part of your game?"

"Not until I've made a couple more moves," I smirked back at him.

Anne returned and the professor and I traded a few old stories, true ones, while we ate. I remembered the list of San Diego P.I.s in my pocket and presented it to Arthur. I asked if he recognized any of the names, and if any of them were known for getting along well with the police.

He knew that by 'getting along' I didn't mean falling down for every cop and handing over cases to them. I needed somebody who was smart enough to trade favors, to get information without giving back more than was needed in kind. He recognized a couple of them and told me Ross Malick was a good bet. "He came out here once when I was helping flush out a liquor ring. He tipped us off to the name of a slippery rum-runner, and we let him peek into the gang boss's bedroom, where his client's wife was spending a lot of time."

I left them without quite finishing my meal or my beer. My burger really was good, but I still wanted to look like I was in a hurry. The Professor would bill me for the meal later.

My afternoon truly was busy. The photo lab had my prints ready as promised. I had four black-and-white postcard size prints each of the dozen-plus exposures I'd left to have developed. A third of them were a series of sunrise pictures I'd made of Tucson from Sentinel Peak. I'd forgotten that was on the roll. It was a shot every tourist in Tucson takes, and now I had three dollars' worth of grayscale copies of it.

The other images were worth that and more. Carolyn's night shot of the deep-faced man was as good as that color film could get. The dumb look on his face, looking into the shadows at a curious sound, was magnified by the low artificial lights and his own distinct features. The daylight exposures of him with the other two fellows outside Universal had usable details to pick from, including a California license plate.

Shade was not plentiful in Tucson but I found some to park under and worked in my car. Three letters I had started that morning got finished and paired up with sets of photo prints. Each letter asked for specific and general information from the recipient about the photo subjects, noting that said subjects probably had criminal histories.

I stopped to get some good stiff envelopes. The expansive downtown drugstore sold those, and screwdrivers, and steel pots (they were out of aluminum), and ice cream. I stopped at the soda counter to check my work and address each envelope.

A short walk through the old presidio got me to the main post office for Tucson. First class postage sent one envelope to northern New Jersey. Another went to Detroit. On a hunch I also paid to send one by international air mail to Ottawa, Ontario. I hoped an old contact from Windsor would remember me, the little boy riding along in his father's squad car during an inter-departmental exchange.

Since I was in the neighborhood I went across the two busy streets that defined downtown Tucson to the small state police office in the federal building. I picked up the paperwork to apply for an Arizona private investigator's license.

Filling out the paperwork would give me something idle to do that evening. I was ready to think about something else before deciding which of many problems I would tangle with the next day.

-16- April 27ᵗʰ (Tuesday), Tucson, AZ

My morning started off in a hot rush. I had neglected to get any sort of envelope for the letter to the Kramer & Hodges law firm. I did expect Anne to take a peek, but it didn't seem sporting if there wasn't at least a little paste glue involved. Shortly after six a.m., not expecting any store to be open, I was trying to flatter a young WAC who had overnight desk duty at the Army's Macauley Field. She sent me off with a short stack of plain white letter covers and a friendly smile. I checked through them in case her phone number happened to have been slipped in, but she wasn't quite that friendly.

As mountains go Sentinel Peak is a pimple on the landscape. But it rises 450 feet from the river that bounds downtown Tucson in barely that long a run to the west. It is the only feature of note for a mile to its west and twenty miles to its east. Those twenty miles include Tucson and the University of Arizona. If you've seen a picture of it, the picture was probably centered on the giant painted "A" that students laid on the mountainside decades ago.

At quarter to seven I parked in a gravel lot in the center of the mountain's flat crater top. I walked over the eastern rise to a popular lookout over the city. An amateur photographer passed me going the other direction. His female companion helped carry his equipment back to their car. It was the same trip I had done a month before.

At five minutes to seven I heard light steps in the gravel behind me. Anne came up quietly to take a spot a few feet away, looking down into the fire-lit city. Morning sun always seems harsher than sunset, and I've never known why.

I made quick work of handing her the freshly sealed envelope and sending her on her way. She affirmed that she'd already fueled up her car, checked the tires, and would be back to meet Professor Arthur.

The sound of Anne's car pulling away and winding down the far side of the mountain was the only sound for a moment. It was replaced by the insistent low gurgle of a light east wind working its way into the crevices of the mountain and every object on it. I lingered at the lookout for a long while. The wind was light but persistent and inescapable. A pale thick crescent moon hung high up in the deep blue post-night sky. The sun was well clear of the distant Rincon Mountains and was putting harsh light onto the city below me. It wasn't hot yet, but there was no indication that anything would stop that sun from toasting the wide valley into another blurry haze that day.

I picked out the roof of a house miles away, one of a hundred on its city block. I thought it must have a dog behind it, lazing in the shade beside its doghouse. As the sun moved overhead the dog would certainly move to the north side of the hut, then the east, staying out of the hot, naked glare.

With Anne occupied, productively, for the next twelve to fourteen hours, I got on with my own business of the day, starting with a late breakfast. Working people were filing out of the downtown diner. Bankers were filing in.

I had nothing to read, and my waitress was neither attractive nor chatty. So I watched the other people. Each of them had a plan for the day. Most probably thought it was somewhat important. A few would be sure that their activities were of utmost priority to the grace of the world. I figured my own work was somewhere in the middle.

I quit breakfasting at two cups of coffee. I picked up another paper cup full from the corner store on the way to my car.

The big library was just open again. I stopped there and went for the out-of-town papers. They had just put out one of the Sunday editions from San Diego. I picked through it in some detail to make sure there was not further news about the dead Mr. Windham. There was none.

It wasn't quite a decent hour in San Diego yet (for an independent gumshoe), so I let my planned phone call wait and went driving again.

122

The directions from Professor Arthur were vague, and I didn't even have the address, but I was sure when I found it. The abandoned service station Anne had been staking out was the only structure like it on or around its block.

It was well built originally, and the building showed few admittances of its late neglect. The two bay doors faced the street, twenty feet back up an asphalt driveway. The gray sheet metal roof rose steeply to a ridge cap that ran perpendicular to the street. A small cluster of shrubs cut into the near corner of the driveway. The nearest neighbors were a small windowless industrial building and a glass front retail store that had sold lawn mower parts when those were available. Neither place showed signs of recent commerce.

I parked across the street and walked up. There had been no rain in a while, not since the wind storm of ten days before at least. I got down close to the ground to look for marks in the dust. Any shapes I saw were fragmented and mixed, but tire and shoe tread patterns showed up well enough in places.

The garage had been visited lately by at least two different vehicles and three different men. There could have been more, and there could have been a change in rubber for either wheels or feet. But if I had to bet I'd put either down as a rare thing under the real scarcity of such goods (that is, it wasn't just arbitrary rationing – tires and shoes truly were scarce).

The bay doors were solid sheet metal except for the top panels which had clear inserts. I had nothing to climb up on to peek inside the panels, but I also would bet that they were blacked out from the inside. The only other door was solid steel and bolted shut.

I walked around back. In the gravel lot behind the place I found nothing but the usual utility hook-ups to the building and a badly curated collection of desert weeds.

The building still had nothing to do with me. It was simply amusing that my temporary associate had stumbled upon something going on there. If I could find somebody who cared about what was happening I might even be able to make a fee-paying case out of it.

I put the place out of my mind, not writing down even what little I had found. It was time to make my phone call. It was also time to get out of the glaring sun. Since I was on the south side of Tucson I cut over to the nearby El Conquistador for a cold drink and an air-conditioned lobby with pay phones.

A hard drink in the middle of the day can be genuinely refreshing and even helpful, if it's not too stiff. There was little risk of getting a stiff drink at the El Con since liquor stocks were being guarded like only daughters until civilian production of booze was okayed again. I brought up the subject as I ordered that drink.

The young bartender quipped, "If I'd known you could make explosives from a liquor still, I'd have built one years ago!" While distilleries had been conscripted into making war goods, including munitions, I didn't think it was a simple as pouring wort into a shell casing.

124

I ate a light lunch at his rail while entertaining his notions of blowing up tree stumps and old trash cans.

Comfortably satiated I went to the phones. Two open courtesy phones sat on a counter next to a pair of private pay phone booths. I took a booth after making a hefty pile of change at the front desk.

An operator came on and asked if my call had military priority. I admitted that it did not. I was told there would be a wait for a circuit, during which I wondered what ever would happen to me if I simply lied to get put through sooner.

After six minutes wait and four rings on the other end of the completed circuit Ross Malick himself answered the phone of Malick & Associates, Investigative Services. I introduced myself, said he'd been referred by a retired cop, and got down to business.

He was already aware of the matter I mentioned, as I'd hoped. "Yes, I read about the Windham murder case. I'm assuming it was a murder, the police statement was vague on the matter. But you calling about it makes me sure."

"I have no idea," I insisted. "I know that I saw him less than ten days before he died, and got made fool of by the people we were working for."

Malick understood what I was after. "So you want to figure out the swindle, but don't want to get wrapped up in the murder case, is that right?"

"There's no murder case, as far as I know." I added coins to the phone, the audible clicks filling the deliberate pause I was taking. "My problem probably has nothing to do with Windham being dead. But to be sure I want to know what the police know."

"Without giving them anything in return?" His voice betrayed more intrigue than exasperation. After a long thought he came back, "The cops have already talked to the family, and this guy was a drifter, close to nobody. I don't think any of them would pony up for an outside investigation. You're not even giving me a premise to work with here."

I offered up the idea I already had half-baked. "Right, but since he's dead, there's an estate to settle. We know it's probably not much, but someone else might think otherwise."

He thought another moment and started warming up to the idea. "Sure, and the probate court will have to do a due diligence search to settle it, however small. I know who arranges those at county, and they usually get farmed out." He was getting happier with every thought. "I could volunteer to pick up this one and become official on the case. It might work."

I wore a tight half grin at the realization of what I'd created, "It might get you paid twice for the same job, you mean!"

I heard a soft chuckle on the other end. He wasn't sore at the accusation; he was talking to another pro at the same game. "Hey, a probate records search doesn't usually include schmoozing the cops for grisly details of the death. And you'll get my best rate on it, out of professional courtesy, of course."

"Of course," I repeated, while wondering, 'best rate for whom?' I agreed to send a retainer by mail and he would get busy on it that day.

The rest of my day was quiet. I didn't see a reason to be up early for the rest of the week, and thought I might be working late. I picked up a little food and took it back to my cottage. I even tried to take a nap, though that never works for me.

Tired of reading newspapers and weekly magazines I jumped all the way over to starting Moby Dick again. I don't really think I'll ever finish it. For the tenth time at least I read Ishmael's enthusiastic recommendations toward the sea and any more minor body of water.

I contemplated the desert around me, which truly was a foreign Earth to me, and thought he may be right to assert that we all want to be by the water. "All men, if they but knew it..." began the passage I thought I had memorized. I never remembered it right, but I say Melville's grammar was always a little out of sorts.

After the usual couple chapters, I put the book down and turned on the radio in my front room. I sipped a little whisky over ice while switching around between evening programs. I thought some people might make a drinking game out of the frequent entreaties to buy bonds or salvage material or donate blood. By any scoring system that's nothing but a quick way to get really drunk and use up a lot of liquor.

I used up my share anyway and finally went to bed.

I woke up too early for having kept myself up past midnight. I had time to kill so I wandered out on foot to find a place to eat farther away than my usual. I picked up two newspapers and read them in detail with no particular purpose.

Eventually I made my way back home, got ready for the day, and left in my car. At ten o'clock I arrived at the Randolph Park Gun Club. I walked in in shirt sleeves. The day's heat had come early.

Professor Arthur and Anne were there to meet me. They were in the small classroom by the range entrance where the professor was giving Anne her basic safety lecture. The premise of the morning session was that she would get some basic firearms training. She admitted to only ever firing a shotgun a couple times, with cousins on a relative's farm as a teenager. We would start her out with my little .38 revolver, using reduced power cartridges Arthur often made for just such occasions.

The real purpose of the meeting was for me to feel out Anne for any reaction to the letter she may have peeked at the day before. I also wanted her thoughts in general about the Zelatoff company. The shooting range provided a public place where it would be difficult for anyone to listen in on us, if, at a stretch, she had talked to anyone else or if Zelatoff had her followed as a routine security measure. We had the place to ourselves that weekday morning hour.

We got Anne kitted out with hearing protection and shoe covers (a hot shell between the toes can be a real nuisance) and went out to a booth. The range was outdoors, but the business end was beneath a covered extension of the building. Shooting toward the east the sun by then was high enough not to blind or to bake us under the high awning.

I didn't try to make conversation until after Anne had gone through a few shot groups. The professor started her out at something less than ten yards. She was predictably nervous, but not out of control like some first timers. She only pointed a live gun back at me and Arthur once before patient correction from the professor established minimum range discipline.

I helped move the target frames out to fifteen yards. The professor and I got into the game. He shot the revolver a few times, explaining details of his stance and grip to Anne. I got up and practiced shooting my 9 mm from a draw several times. It was mostly for show, but I really did want the practice.

Anne fired again then the professor took a turn with my pistol. He took his time making close groups. I started trying to debrief Anne. "So, everything go OK yesterday?"

She looked back at me in a quick start. "Oh, yes. Yes, it went fine." She looked back between the professor and me a couple times, then asked, "Was the lawyer supposed to send anything back with me?"

"No, he's just getting started on the case." Professor Arthur was really getting dialed in. If I let him shoot much more he would outshoot me, on my own favorite gun. I started the planned segue, "You're shooting pretty good. You know, if you wanted to keep at it, you could do OK at this business." It felt as contrived as it was, but seemed to work.

"You think so?" She looked over, then turned her whole body to face me. Her satisfied grin was barely suppressed.

"Sure do. Do you think they miss you at Zelatoff?"

She came back quickly with a ready answer. "They can go to hell for all I care!" I had never seen Anne animated or profane. "The place is crooked somehow; I just know it. There's secret files, and sealed messages, and places we weren't supposed to go." She stopped to look up into the corners of the half-enclosed space we were in. "And they've got television cameras everywhere. Can you think what that must have cost?"

I didn't wonder about the cost of cameras. I wondered if her prepared statement about Zelatoff was from genuine angst she'd felt while working there, or a smokescreen, telling me what I wanted to hear. I let it go as it was, and we talked about trigger pull and the cost of ammo until I made my busy excuses to leave.

I would owe the professor also for the actual cost of ammo.

I could have used some groceries for my place, but I had little tolerance right then to deal with ration points and coupon books. I picked up a couple restaurant sandwiches packed to go and hauled them back. I needed to camp out next to the phone for the rest of the day. If phones in the rooms rang too long calls got switched to the front desk. I didn't want to be chasing messages.

Afternoon radio shows were my company for the first few hours. All my letters out had asked for a call back during the afternoon (my time) as soon as there was any information worth sharing. The first call came from the lawyer in San Diego; it was the same attorney with Kramer and Hodges.

"Mister Guyon, I have some initial results for you. You said to call first thing. Thank you for the advance payment, by the way."

"No problem. Go ahead and give me the quick summary." I was sure to be billed for the long-distance call, by the minute, on top of the lawyer's time.

"OK... I can start with Universal Spline and Coupler, since that will be quick. There's nothing. It's a real company, incorporated in California, but there's nothing in the state record to follow after. Fischer, Metzler, and Wislavic filed the corporate papers, writing

131

itself in as the representative of record, lead shareholder, and primary addressee."

I hummed an acknowledgment so the young lawyer could continue.

"I didn't think you'd settle for that though, so we dug a little more, pulling the obligatory corporate filings. They slipped up. They don't technically have to list an accountant and auditor in their filings, unless it's a traded stock, but someone did, to put a gloss of legitimacy on things I suppose. The accounting is audited by Fischer, Metzler, and Wislavic, of course. But the actual accounting is done by Johnson and Company – which was acquired by Fischer, et al. just two years ago."

I spoke up at that bit. "Isn't that against some kind of ethical code?"

"You bet it is. Thing is, unless there's a shareholder to complain about it, nobody's going to check up on it." I heard papers rustling as he turned to the next records. "Do you expect there are really any other shareholders?"

"I'd bet all but that one first share are held by some arm of Zelatoff." I had my own notepad out now, hoping for some actual information.

"Well I have the records for Zelatoff in front of me now, or a summary that is. It's a big company now, you know."

I gave a knowing grunt again.

"We only have the complete records for California so far, but that's probably it. A first look says everything the company used to have on the east coast was closed up neatly and legally dissolved. Here in California the company is organized as a holding company with five operating companies running each of five locations."

"They're all closely held. Mr. Zlatkov is the president of all the companies. Only about five percent of the holding company was ever floated to investors, and not on the open market."

I asked, without much hope, "So if we set accountants on the available statements, what could they get out of them as far as what the business is up to?"

"Not much. There's nothing but a generic balance sheet and overall profit and loss statement. If you're looking for something unusual or shady it would have to be a million dollars a month to even register."

"One more thing," he added. "That plate you gave us is on a 1937 Ford van, and it's a Zelatoff pool vehicle, registered as industrial equipment." He said it with finality. There was no next page in his stack.

"Well, that's that then. So let me just ask your opinion." He said to shoot. "The set up at Universal, is that unusual enough to point to something shady? And I mean criminal."

"If you mean is it cause enough for police to search the place, no, not at all. There's nothing illegal, yet, about hiding the details of one's business. If you mean does it look suspicious, then hell yeah.

I thanked him though it didn't help much, since I was already suspicious as hell. I confirmed my address for the complete report to be sent to me. If they were any good at their business, and it seemed like they were, a bill would be the first page.

Another couple hours later Carolyn called. I was chewing on a slightly stale sandwich, not noticing that it had gotten to our prearranged time.

"Hello, darling," she said with uncomfortable sensuality. It took me another moment to remember that she was supposed to call from a lobby pay phone. It was probably unnecessary, but it seemed a sensible precaution for us not to dial direct from hotel room phone to motel room phone.

"Hey, kid." There was no reason for me to play along. "What's up?"

"Nothing much. I've been getting out and seeing the area, shopping in some different departments." I hoped she wasn't taking chances digging too deeply around Zelatoff.

"Did you find anything new?"

"Oh, no, it's pretty boring here, just the same stores as everywhere else. But, you remember that little place we visited for dessert on our last weekend getaway?"

"That'd be Universal. OK."

"Right. Well, I heard that they're getting another shipment of the special dish you wanted to try, a whole truck of it."

I had expected that stolen trucks went to Universal to unload and launder the material back into Zelatoff. Whatever she had found, that cinched it. "Yes, that is great news. But when?"

"The notice I read said they would have a special running starting sometime next week. So do you think we can go back?"

"I'll need to know the actual date. We might want to make a party out of it, and I need to send out invitations." Now I was playing along anyway.

"Of course, sweetie. I'll see what I can find out about the menu. Talk to you soon, darling!" She was laying it on sticky sweet now.

I hurried to add, "Just don't annoy the chef too much by asking about his business."

"Bye-bye!" She blew me a kiss and hung up.

So another truck would be diverted to Universal, soon. I was thinking of how to be sure we could meet the truck when it got to San Diego. That left open the question of what to do once we found it. I could bring a van full of thugs and crash the party at Universal, but then what?

Or, maybe the load would never get there at all. Another plan began to hatch.

## -18- April 28th (Wednesday), Tucson, AZ

Again I attempted to catch an evening nap. It didn't take. I laid on my back watching a movie on the ceiling, one with good guys and bad guys and a clever story where everything works out in the end. That was all imaginary, as none of my current problems and complications lined up that neatly.

I was going to need more help, cheap and quick. Placing a want ad for associates was a poor option on both counts. I had one good lead to follow, and that night I would get a better idea where it led.

My imaginary movie hadn't gotten to the part where the good guy gets the girl when I decided it was time to leave. Long after sunset the pavement still radiated the heat of the day. I tossed my jacket and hat in the passenger seat ahead of me.

I drove indirectly toward where I had seen my old acquaintance Smithy tending gas pumps. I came out onto the highway a half mile from his station and drove by at a casual speed. The place was dark, with no cars out front and only a few vehicles back behind the building, in a fenced yard like how some garages keep customers' cars.

The moon would not rise until nearly four a.m. (I had checked on that). The only light on the building came from two streetlamps each almost a hundred yards east or west along the main highway and one other fainter light just as far up a near side street. I motored on another quarter mile or so and turned on to the next highway. Just around that corner was one of the few operating used car lots to be found. I mixed my car into the inventory and unloaded my gear from the trunk.

I had put higher sensitivity film in the camera, but thought about the lighting conditions around the garage and decided it was a lost cause. The camera stayed packed. My chosen kit consisted of a light folding chair, small binoculars, and my old overcoat, which happened to be black. I didn't carry a gun. It was one less thing to have to explain to the police if some concerned citizen saw me prowling around.

I stayed in a block from the commercial frontage, off the main highway. This put me in front of cozy houses, owned by citizens each proud of their own private piece of the world. I walked as casually as one can while creeping through a neighborhood near midnight carrying spy gear and a trench coat.

Along the short walk I saw only one bedroom window lit, through a drawn curtain. No one noticed the stranger on the sidewalk. The greatest risk of the job having passed, I came out to the highway again and set up shop.

The wide-spaced street lighting left me shadowy patches to pick from. I chose an alley between a dry cleaner and a closed-up trophy shop. The spot was a bit east of the garage across the road. From there I could see most of the back part of the L-shaped building.

My eyes adjusted to the dark. I watched and waited. Cars drove by not more often than two an hour. One police cruiser rolled by slowly but paid me no mind. I had the dark overcoat draped over me like a blanket. The air behind me gave some relief from the heat of the previous day which had only just started to take leave of the city.

I risked sticking my arm out into the light a couple times to read my wrist watch. It was near two a.m. that I got some action.

Two cars rolled up together. They maneuvered around the fuel pumps to stop in front of the service bays. I was unsure of the makes, but one was an older style coupe and the other a larger and newer-model sedan.

Someone got out of the smaller car and opened one of the four bay doors, second from the right, which had not had a car in it for service the two days earlier. From inside he opened the last overhead door on the right. The larger car pulled into the empty work space. The ambulatory man brought in his own car and closed both doors.

Through the field glasses I watched nothing happen for a few more minutes. Then a light came on in the back part of the building. Facing the rear lot from that section were a smaller overhead door and a single man door farther to the rear. Neither door admitted any light from inside. The light I saw came from a window high up in the near end of the gabled building section, above the single-story flat-roofed front. The window had no glass, just a solid cover that was swung wide open. I guessed it was the only ventilation for that rear building with the doors closed.

From that one window I could tell that the space was one big open room, high ceilinged and well-lit. Occasionally a faint shadow moved over the rafters, telling me some of the lights were mounted low in the room and people were moving around in front of them.

A third vehicle pulled in and night-blinded me through the binoculars as it made a full turn around the gas pumps before heading to the back entrance. Another man got out and opened the rear door of his sedan. He loaded up his arms with three boxes, each less than a foot long on all sides. He shut the car door with a foot and approached the building. He worked a hand free at the wrist to grasp the handle and opened the door.

A flood of light lit him for a moment and I wished I'd brought the camera. He stepped inside, coming back half a minute later with empty arms to close the door.

I waited. I watched more shadows move in the light. A while later all movement stopped. I waited a bit more and decided to take a chance on that being the whole party for the evening. I ditched my stuff and ran across the deserted road lanes.

I stopped in front of the main garage. I couldn't see inside to get better details or plate numbers from the cars newly parked there.

But in the still night air I heard a sound. From the open end window, I caught a rhythmic mechanical noise. A soft flapping and whirring rolled through a steady cycle every two or three seconds, with a few less regular sharp clicks and claps to season the bland background music. The sound was not familiar to me.

I walked quietly around the front building section, hoping to get close to the third car. I rounded the last corner and had the car in sight when the whirring stopped. A voice called out something and another answered. I didn't wait around to find out what they said.

I made a quick check of the road and dashed back to my hiding spot. I sat down again and got my heart rate calmed in time to see the three men exit. One held the door while the other two carried out boxes, larger this time but clearly not as heavy. Two at a time they put twelve boxes into the car's trunk.

They went back inside, the light got shut off, and all three left the ways they had come. I was not tempted to try to follow the loaded car, though I could have sprinted back to my car and probably picked it up in a few blocks. Trying to follow at night in the deserted city was an easy way to get burned. I didn't want to scare them off and I didn't care what they were making or where it went anyway.

I called it a night and stalked my way back through the quiet neighborhood. I drove straight home.

## -19- April 29th (Thursday), Tucson, AZ

I slept well and not too late. I made a few notes about my late night excursion then went out to get a few things done. I got fed, had my ration of coffee, and finally got to the bank.

The bank didn't have exactly good news, but I could go on not having a paying client for a comfortable while longer. I paid another month's rent on my motel cottage, checking that there weren't any old messages waiting for me.

The phone was ringing as I re-entered my front room. Sergeant Joseph Halpin of the New Jersey State Police Sussex Station was happy to have caught me. "You said to call in the afternoon, Nick, but I had a free minute so I gave it a try."

Halpin had been a Passiac County deputy when I met him. He would have been a detective there but the sheriff needed a desk to put his nephew behind. They let Joe do some investigating for fun. He made it into the State Police when the war came and the recruit pool dried up. That was fine with the sheriff – he had several sisters and another nephew was graduating college that year.

"It's good luck you caught me," I told Joe. "I'm going to run out this afternoon, it turns out. So can you tell me anything about the guys I sent you?"

"I sure can," Sergeant Halpin started enthusiastically. "I passed around the pictures and two of them lit up faces right away. They've both made the rounds through different jails around here."

"I figured so, and I guessed that they came out of the old gangs out your way." I finally put down the things I was holding and sat down by the phone base.

"You nailed it, pal. It seems you've taken a couple bad apples off our hands, and I've got plenty more to send you if I could." He paused for a second. "These first two were pretty small time before. Does it look like they're stepping up in the world now?" I said that they were.

"Yeah, them and every other small-time hood and bootlegger," he continued. "People want to think it all ended in '34. They don't see the army of crooks we made, all organized and big-business, each of them looking for a chance to do his own thing."

"Well they certainly have their chance now, don't they?" I asked the wall.

"They sure do," he answered the rhetorical question. "The small fries before are all 15 years older and taking charge of things now. We're swatting 'em like flies over here and can't keep up."

"Well keep on sending 'em out west," I encouraged. "I could use the business." I heard a familiar hearty chuckle. "Now how about those first two I've adopted from you?"

Halpin proceeded to tell me what he had found out about the two men I had seen at Universal Spline & Coupler with the deep-faced man.

"Slim" Hackett, Joe didn't have the full name yet, used to drive for the Maxim syndicate, one of the smaller ones, run by Bulgarian immigrants. He ran the overland routes through upstate New York, hauling back Canadian whisky from lake shore pickups. He never got caught 'wet.' Nothing ever stuck but for a few speeding tickets. He stayed in northern New Jersey when he wasn't working.

The other guy had a longer record. Bernie Rokoszak was strictly muscle. He might have worked for the same gang. He got picked up for several bar fights in New Jersey. One time he slugged an undercover state cop. That got him locked up and his place searched. They found enough cased booze to get him locked up for a while, but he never said where it came from.

"Wait, he slugged a cop? I'm sure he got a little uglier on the way to jail," I interjected.

"He was already ugly," Joe assured me, "if you're worried about how his face resisted arrest."

"Fair enough," I concluded. "But what about the really ugly guy, in the one night photo?"

"Nothing on him," Joe answered conclusively. "If he ever ran around here nobody I know dealt with him. I put a note in to the FBI office, but you know they're pretty busy. They seem to think there are German spies running around."

I suggested fencing off Pennsylvania and locking up all the Germans, since we just did that to all the Japanese in California. Joe thought Roosevelt might worry about carrying Pennsylvania in the next election.

"Probably so. Now what about the other guy, the one with no picture?"

Since I had a name for Nigel Thompson matching records had come up quickly. It was his real name. He was New York City born and had come up as an enforcer-for-hire through the New York gangs.

Eventually he took over distribution operations for a new crew that was making headway into Maryland. Somebody talked and Nigel got caught with a load. He did four years of his sentence but never told who had bankrolled his operation.

I thanked Joe and we wrapped up. He explained that if I wanted copies of the files there was a records fee. I grunted acknowledgement and he said for me they'd send a bill with the records.

Before he hung up I threw up one more name. "Hey, remember Mike Minervini, the informant we used sometimes?"

"Smithy? Sure I do," Joe confirmed. "I never was sure if I got it straight from him, but he told good stories."

"Yeah, same here. Well he turned up here in Tucson, pumping gas. What do you think of that?"

Joe paused a moment to compose a quip, "I'd keep an eye on what else he's pumping. He'll fill your head with Cracker Jack and keep the prize."

I let Sergeant Halpin go and scratched out a few more notes. All he had told me didn't really give me much new information. It just proved me right on a few suppositions. Of course it really was new information, and quite valuable, but people tend to discount what they think they already know.

I sat down to read and kill a little more time. I would return to visit Smithy, and I didn't expect he worked a morning shift at the service station.

Near two o'clock I headed out again toward the station. I looked over details of the commercial strip in the daylight for the first time.

A few of the retail and service shops were perpetually busy. A third of them were shuttered. The war time economy, if it could be called an economy, offered some an embarrassment of riches and left others simply embarrassed.

Typical of greater Tucson, and any spreading desert community, most buildings were one or two story, with plenty of parking and minimal landscaping.

Near Smithy's station the only decoration was colored gravel islands with a few struggling shrubs.

The clean new building had only a large paved lot around it. I rolled up the generous ramp to an island which paralleled the building front. I pulled forward to the second of two double-sided fuel pumps. I wasn't out of the car yet before Smithy was on his way out of the building to wait on me.

"Hey, Nick, good to see you again so soon. You been driving around a lot, I 'spose. Been working?"

I reached back into the car for my jacket as I answered. "Yes, I'm on a case now. It's had me poking around all over." I fished a B-series gas ration coupon book out of the inside jacket pocket. "I might have to take another drive again soon. So, why dontcha' just fill it up."

I thumbed the genuine ration book, my last one, while he got the fuel pump going. He asked me what I thought about some new movie, which I hadn't seen. He didn't ask anything else, as it isn't normally a long job.

The silence stretched out, the clicks of the gas pump getting louder, as eight gallons, then ten, then twelve went into the twin tanks of my Lincoln. At fifteen Smithy asked if I was sure I wanted him to top it off. At twenty he stopped and looked under the car to make sure there wasn't a leak spilling fuel all over the pavement.

He saw me grinning at him when he got up. Without a word he got back on the hose and kept

147

filling. With twenty-six-and-a-half gallons dispensed gurgling was heard up the filler tube and he stopped the flow expertly without wetting my car's paint.

I handed over the coupon book. "Keep the change." There was enough paper left in the book to cover 30 gallons of gas. I took out my wallet to count out bills for the cash part of our transaction.

He flipped open the coupon book and made a quick count. He held it up close and turned it in the sunlight before stopping to peer at me over the edge of the booklet. "Sorry, Nick, don't mean no offense, but it's kinda a habit to check for fakes these days."

"No offense taken. Go ahead, look it over. It's the real deal." I waited with cash in hand for him to inspect the book.

The numbers written and printed on the paper didn't mean much to Smithy. He felt the book more than look at it, catching the impressions of the different printing types used and the raise of the perforations. He probably wasn't an expert counterfeiter, but he knew more than a typical gas station attendant. His fingertips had a little red around the stubborn blue ink that day.

"Well sure, Nick," he said to me as he tucked the book into a shirt pocket, "of course it's the real deal." But why're you giving it to me? With the 'C' sticker on your car I could let go whatever gas you needed."

I handed over the cash. "Right, and then when your logs get turned in at some point my number winds up on a list and someone comes asking why I do so much preaching out-of-state. That book will tie back to Gladys

148

from Albuquerque and the Plymouth she sold a few months ago. Any problem selling Gladys the gas?"

"No trouble at all, Nick! You come back any time. Just, say, lemme know ahead so I can have enough gas, OK? I may run out before the next truck this week."

"I'll be sure to take care of you," I said with the reassuring emphasis of a finger pointed at his chest. "Now, if you could get me a deal on a set of tires for this machine, I'd be mighty interested."

He laughed it off. "You and me both! If I had a line on rubber I wouldn't be here counting paper coupons all day."

I shook his hand to say goodbye, but didn't let it go. I pulled it up closer to my eyes, stained fingernail edges up. "Speaking of paper coupons, I think you might have more blank ones stashed somewhere." I let the arm drop and looked directly into his tensing face. "I'm going to need more, if they're any good."

Smithy looked at the nails of the hand I'd let go then back up at me. "Allright, since you seem on the level, I'll tell you; I think I can get what you need. This ink," he held up the hand again, "isn't from gas rations, but I know who can get you some. Is that all you need?"

He gave me more information than he needed to. "I could use more coffee, but mostly the gas stamps."

"OK, Nick, no problem. You just wind up back here at closing time night after tomorrow, Saturday, and I'll bring a few books to pick from. Can you make it?"

"I'll be back," is all I said as I got into my car and pulled out onto the sun-baked street.

It was evening when I wound up back at my place. An easterly breeze did nothing to cut through the steady heat and I thought it would feel good to drive around.

I took in the contrast of the repetitive suburban cityscape against the background of the omnipresent mountains. The city had developed and would continue to evolve, while the mountains would never change. Yet it was forever the city that would look monotonous next to that intractable majesty.

A note was tacked to my door declaring that an urgent message was waiting for me. I could hear my room phone ringing inside so I went to it first.

"Oh, thank goodness, finally!" exclaimed Carolyn . I've been trying you since three."

She should have been at work then, her time or mine. Before taking any details I had presence of mind to ask, "Where are you calling from?"

"I'm at a pay phone," she said, "outside a grocery three blocks from the hotel."

That was exactly what I needed to hear. We could both speak freely from there on. She explained quickly.

Since cluing me in on the next truck to Universal she had been digging deeper, carefully. She had thought ahead enough to start acting a little sickly and spending more time in the ladies' room. If she would need to sneak a peek at some private mail she would smuggle it into the restroom with her to have a little time with it and not be watched. She even thought to ask the other women where nearby one would go to pick up medicine for 'ladies' relief' to further button up her cover and to give her a way out in a few days.

Twice she had a chance to open something marked private and confidential. The first time she was delivering mail and simply interrupted her rounds, taking the whole cart with her to the restroom. Hot water steamed open an envelope to reveal an invitation of Mister Zlatkov, founder of Zelatoff, to a congressman's fund raising gala.

The second time an envelope turned up for Nigel Thompson, closed with a tie string instead of paste sealed. It wasn't in Carolyn's mail pile; it had just been placed on the desk of the office manager after a courier left it. Carolyn brazenly walked off with it and mixed it into the regular mail.

She got a look at the contents but was caught putting it back on the manager's desk. "I think he believed me, Nick, that I just found it mixed in with my stack, but I can't be sure that he won't check up on it."

"Anyway, after that I complained about particularly bad cramps," she continued, "and left early to find a drugstore. I tried to call you from there, and from near every bus stop on the way back after work." She went on to describe what was in the letter.

The letter was mostly a hand-drawn map. A few localities were lettered and notes indicated what was to happen at each mark. Carolyn had roughly copied the map and some of the notes.

The next truck heist was to start exactly like the last one, near Radium Springs. The new "security man" was a fellow new to El Paso. A new driver hadn't been hired so one of the "the boys" would drive solo. The "drop point" was to be in Arizona this time, on the north end of the great Apache reservation.

Mister Thomson was to phone the usual number if he wanted any changes. If he didn't the job was set for Tuesday night.

Carolyn sighed at the end of her story, "I do hope it helps, Nick. I really do have a sick gut after sneaking around like that."

"I hope it helps, too." I finally threw my stuff on the sofa and sat down at my little desk. "I'm not sure yet what we're going to do about it, but it's time to get you out of there." I thought about that another moment and told her, "You'll get an urgent call at work tomorrow. It will mean you have to leave on short notice, and don't know when you'll be able to come back."

I figured Anne would have to be sent packing, as well. That would require yet another story, which I would leave to the professor to invent. I told Carolyn to get whatever she wanted at the bar. She told me that she already had and we hung up.

I checked with the motel office and got the urgent message from earlier. *Dinner party set for Tuesday night. Hope you have time to inform other guests.*

-20- April 30th (Friday), Tucson, AZ

I called Professor Arthur early. He was not at home; he was not at the range. Finally, I got a call back from him near 10 a.m. He had picked up some dark sand from a custom stoneworker he knew and took it to Anne's regular stakeout location. He had showed her how to spread it out thin on the pavement so it's not noticeable underfoot but leaves tracks that one can read in the daylight. He had decided she didn't need to be up late watching the place any more.

"You're absolutely right," I confirmed. "In fact, you need to send her back."

"Oh, do I? Last I talked to her she was practically in tears over a letter that came from Albuquerque. She's already in a mood." He tried to be annoyed but accepted this next chore readily enough. "OK, then, what happened?"

"Carolyn hit the jackpot," I enthused. I didn't give him all the details right away, but explained that she might get burned if she stayed any longer. Anne had served her purpose – and been paid – and we owed Zelatoff their employee back.

"Are you sure Zelatoff will want her back?" Arthur Mason might have got somewhat attached to his enthusiastic charge. "Can we at least offer her a decent severance?"

He wasn't wrong. I moaned an OK then spelled it out, "She's been here two weeks. Give her an extra week, but make it sound painful. Tell her the client we had on this job backed out and we're not even sure we're going to get paid."

He said he would take care of it and I knew that he would. I grabbed my hat and jacket and got moving.

I went uptown, northwest of the university. Marilyn Torge's all-purpose apartment building was just off Oracle Road. I went through what was, so far as I know, the only roundabout to be found connecting major American highways for a thousand miles. Carolyn's place was there, and I was hoping she had left my name as a contact in case anything came up with her kids.

Mrs. Torge was there. She came out from the rear of the building to greet me in the cramped lobby. "Good morning, Mister Guyon. Don't I recognize you from somewhere?"

"From somewhere around town, at a play maybe," I offered. "I think it was Rigoletto they had going last fall."

She showed me into a small office to the side. The building was solidly built but it was built many years

154

before, stubbornly modest and difficult to upgrade. She turned an old fashioned light switch on the wall and we sat across a small dark table.

"I understand you've come asking about Carolyn Barnes' children, is that correct?"

"Yes, that's pretty much right." The room was closed in and airless. I set my hat on the table and opened my jacket.

She looked me over with a slight squint. "You should know that the children are at school. This evening they will join the other children at our evening program. Then one of the girls will see that they get to bed in their apartment. I do have your name from Miss Barnes, but of course that doesn't mean I can just let you in."

"Oh, no. Of course." I waved off whatever she might be thinking. "I'm sure the children are fine, and I don't need to see anything. Carolyn is out of town working for me, actually, and I need for her to come back."

Mrs. Torge did not act confused or even curious. "Very well. What do you need done?"

"I need for the other people she's with to believe that she has to come back on a sudden emergency. They don't need to know that she has children, just that there's a sudden illness in the family and she's needed." I saw a modest nod from the rotund woman. "It would be best if it came from a legit source, directly from you if you please."

155

"It's a simple enough task. But Mister Guyon, why me? You could hire any woman off the street to make this call."

I didn't answer her question. I fished my check book from my jacket. "It's almost the first. I can pay Carolyn's rent and day care for May now." She was looking down at the check I was about to write. "And another twenty dollars for your extra effort."

"When does this call need to be made?" she asked, without looking up from the check.

I told her any time this afternoon would be good. I verified the total with her, signed the check, and gave her a note with the call details on it.

Mrs. Torge walked me to the door. In parting she said, "I'm sure now that I do remember you. And the only play running here last fall was Merchant of Venice. Rigoletto is an opera."

I put my hat on over a lingering look back toward the entrepreneurial woman. I walked on to my car without another word.

I took in a generous lunch, with two bottles of beer. Back at my place I finally got in a successful nap. I would be up late again and would be glad to have the rest. I needed to be sharp that night.

I was awake again around six in the evening. I relaxed the best I could, keeping my mind idly occupied. Music from the radio ran through a jumble of styles as I fussed over the knob. I spun away from busy talk and news any time it came on.

After dark I got myself busy. I laid out my guns and went through a practiced routine of inspecting and cleaning them. I showered and put on fresh clothes. I swallowed one neat shot of bourbon. I left.

Ten minutes later I was circling the block where Smithy's service station had been busy the night before. In another two minutes I was pulling up behind the building right up to the rear door.

I backed my car up to the building and left the engine running. I got out. The soft mechanical noise from before was humming again from inside.

I tried the door handle. It was not locked. I was blind as to what was inside, where the men were, or how I'd be received. I felt the 9 mm snugly holstered under my left shoulder. I traced the outline of the little .38 revolver in my right jacket pocket. I opened the door and walked in like I owned the place.

My first bit of luck was that Smithy saw me first. "Nick!" he called out to me from the center of the room, "You was supposed to come tomorrow!"

My second bit of luck was that all four men in the room had their hands full feeding or working or unloading a complicated printing machine. The biggest one, a hairy Greek the size of a P.T. boat was frozen with a giant spool of gold foil paper in his meaty hands. "Smithy, you know dis guy?" he yelled from the right end of the noisy machine.

My third bit of luck was that Smithy decided we were still pals. "Sure, sure." He put down the brush and pot of red ink he had been using to keep wet a well-used

157

drum. "Nick's all right, don't sweat it." A slender man in rolled up sleeves put down the stack of cut labels he had just lifted from the left end of the machine and watched me with his arms crossed. His shoulder holster was out in the open and bulging with a fat .45.

"Shut the door, will ya?" said the fourth man in the room, though he was already walking around the machine to do it himself. I got the door closed myself before he bolted it shut behind me. This last man was of medium height and heavy build and still had a suit jacket on inside the stifling room, closed off from the night air. He was in charge.

He looked at me closely as he asked, "OK, Smithy, who is this guy?"

Wiping his hands with a rag that had already been used too many times Smithy answered, "This is Nick Guyon. He's from back east where I used to run. He hit me up yesterday for some gas books. I said sure, but we was supposed to meet out front tomorrow."

The boss never broke his stare on me. "So what brings you here tonight then, Mister Guyon?"

I answered him in kind, "Smithy, who is this guy yelling in my face?" The boss's eyes narrowed but he backed away some, glancing at Smithy before fixing again on me.

Smithy didn't miss a beat. "This is the guy I told you about, Nick, the owner. He brought me out to work here, just like I said. I would figure you knew what kind of work, not just pumping gas."

158

"The name's George," the older man cut Smithy off. "Just George, for now. Enough crap -- what are you after?"

"George," I said to the irritated man with an outstretched hand, "I'm Nick Guyon and I'm here to do business with you." The man's eyes, three inches below mine, never broke contact as he eventually put out his hand to meet mine in a firm grip.

I stepped into the room. Most of it was taken up by the printing apparatus, an assemblage of sections of different ages functionally joined together, spanning over thirty feet long. A row of deep shelves on the back wall held printing supplies, clear glass liquor bottles (empty), and broken down cardboard boxes.

I walked, was half-herded, to the far side of the long machine. I stayed standing. The big Greek and the thinner man stood near either end of the machine. George took a seat on the only padded chair next to a small table with a few papers and a notepad on it. Smithy pulled a shop stool back from the machine and sat a little bit behind and to the side of his boss.

"I have a job," I explained. "It's hot. It will pay well. It needs five or six men to pull off." George mostly listened to me for the next many minutes. He liked my pitch well enough. But he would be supplying most of the muscle – he expected most of the profit. I couldn't argue. My initial offer of 60% got negotiated up to 85% of net. I had hoped to keep it at 80%. I was at least able to make very clear that nobody got paid until what we stole got sold.

I hadn't got into the details yet when the slender man made a connection. "Hey, Smithy, isn't this the guy you told us about, who got a load stolen out from under him? It was in the paper, wasn't it?"

I let Smithy answer, "I don't know for sure, but somebody said that was Nick." He looked around at the other men then back at me. "So, Nick, was that you?"

I made modest effort to defend my honor. "It wasn't like in the paper, be sure of that. Somebody played a rotten trick on me. And that's exactly why I'm here. I want to steal back what they stole from me."

"What who stole?" George asked. He sounded unsure of my sanity. "What was stolen a month ago has to be split up all over the place by now."

I gave him a quick version of my theory on Zelatoff stealing their own loads. The whole band of low-level crooks thought it was a grand idea, in a 'why didn't I think of it first' way. "Is it an insurance play, asked Smithy?"

"Could be, but I don't think so. I can only guess, but I think they just want more material than the government will let them have." I had leaned back against the machine and just then realized the back of my jacket was probably covered in ink.

While I was looking at my hands and twisting my coat around to see the back side the big Greek laughed out loud, "So they can sell more stuff right back to the government! I loves it." He pointed at a blue spot behind me, "I have cleaner for that. Come over here."

I laid out more details of the plan over the next hour. I assured them that local police were taken care of, that I could get the municipal props we needed, and that I had a place to let our haul cool off. From the start George latched quickly onto the appeal of taking from someone who couldn't report the theft to any authorities. We shared a bottle of real whisky and I learned a bit about them and their current operation.

The press was running labels of popular whisky and gin brands. They got put on glass bottles close to the shapes of the ones used by the real distilleries. The empty bottles were boxed up and supplied to contemporary bootleggers who put whatever they wanted in the bottles. "You understand, I hope," emphasized George, "that nothing illegal happens here. It is up to my customer what he does with these... decorative bottles." He seemed to sincerely doubt that anyone would ever cut cheap gin with toxic industrial alcohol and colorants to pass it off as aged whisky.

George Zografos had done well during prohibition in New York and taken his money west, like Smithy had said. His game back in the day was not in bootlegging but in selling supplies to the small-time distillers. He was selling shovels during a gold rush.

The big Greek, Stefano, had driven speedboats for the rum runners. Then he did the tourist boat tours out of Atlantic City, much slower and in the daylight. He couldn't swim and was happy finally to have a job on dry land.

The slender man, August, was the only one recruited locally. I got less of his story, but he had been in Mexico more than a couple times during and after prohibition.

In his notebook George wrote out the list of what we would need. A variety of lumber went down next to shovels and two heavy-duty mechanic's jacks. "I have the jacks here, but of course I have to record some expense for their use." I okayed it but moaned inside. It was a blessing and a curse to work with a real pro at his own gig.

We agreed that the scheme would work with six guys, including me, plus my local associate (the unnamed Professor Arthur) who would handle storing the loot. One of George's mechanics would join us as a shovel man.

The job was set for the following Tuesday night, on a quiet dirt road twenty miles west of Alpine, Arizona.

-21- May 1st (Saturday), Tucson, AZ

I was going to need Arthur Mason to trust me, a
lot. Certainly I already called him a fast friend and had
counted on him to handle some iffy business, but what I
had coming up next was downright dirty. If things went
badly he'd have only his reputation to rely on to talk his
way past a long line of tough characters asking tough
questions. I would have to rely on his reputation, too, to
vouch for my own suspicious character.

I debated how much to tell the professor about the
plan and decided that giving up everything was the only
option.

The El Con had a show that night, a hot ticket for
its relatively small ballroom. Vaughn Monroe was doing
a short tour with a small band, making "V disc"
recordings where they could. I chewed on the ear of the
manager I knew best, dropping the professor's name to
secure three tickets (at full face price). Carolyn would
join us. Professor Arthur would get to see at least one
other part of my motley team, by far the most charming
part.

Carolyn had come back on the very first bus that morning. She would have come overnight if they ran a redeye on that route. She was sore at me for really scaring her, having Mrs. Torge call her to say there was trouble. She said she understood why I did it, to make her sudden exit from Zelatoff look completely genuine, but I wasn't sure that she had really let me off the hook.

I dressed myself the best I knew how for a real night out and went to pick up Carolyn. She came down into the building lobby looking like a hundred grand, if not a million bucks. Some items she was wearing I had seen before. Her hair style might have involved a little more effort than something I'd seen another night. The details were lost on me; I just knew she looked great.

I had presence of mind to ask about her kids. They were "fine," and had gotten into the public school for most of the last two weeks, which cut down what she'd had to pay for day care.

"Do you think we'll be staying in Tucson for a while now?" She asked. "I need to know what to tell them."

'Them' it turned out was a pair of old ladies Mrs. Torge had cajoled out of retirement to work a daycare in another of her husband's old buildings. Business was already good and with summer approaching they expected to stay busy.

"I will have to run out of town a couple times next week, at least," I answered. "You can hang back here and take care of this end if that works better for you. Just stay close to the phone, OK?" It occurred to me that it was time to pay her again, but I didn't have that much cash left on me. It would have to wait until Monday.

"That I can do. Oh, here..." she reached into her simple modern-style hand bag to produce an envelope. She handed the envelope over to me. "I got paid for the first two weeks by Zelatoff on my way out."

I held the envelope for a minute. She had earned the pay, though she was on salary for me, too. It solved an immediate problem anyway. I handed the envelope back. "Count out your next week's pay from me. Then split the rest." There wasn't a lot left over, but my share would be enough to cover me buying her dinner again that night.

I drove over to the El Conquistador, pulling around the west end of the main hotel to park by the rear lounge entrance. It was the kind of night I might have used a valet, but they didn't do that anymore.

We were two minutes early. Arthur Mason was already there, seated at a three-foot-square table by the back wall of the lounge. I presented Miss Carolyn Barnes and presumed that he was suitably impressed.

The professor was annoyed that I had got us a table outside the main dining room. He was placated by a waiter who reminded us that on show nights the full menu was available in the lounge.

"OK, Nick," he started in on me, "you got us set back here away from everyone and brought your partner along. What is it you want to talk about?" Before I could answer he added, "And she's way too good for you, in case you were wondering. OK, go ahead."

Carolyn laughed politely as I started my speech. "I'm going to owe you for a big favor soon, several favors in fact. I thought I'd take us out as a down payment on paying you back."

A round of drinks was set down as the professor reminded me, "You're already in deep to me, last I checked the score. But it's been fun so far. Anne says goodbye, by the way. She was going to head up to Albuquerque to sort something out. She didn't say if she would try back at Zelatoff or not."

Carolyn grinned wickedly at that bit. At my prompting she opened up and explained to Arthur about Anne having a two-timing man in Albuquerque. He was more sympathetic but still found humor in the turn.

I checked that the waiter was not hovering nearby and got right to the key points of the current situation. "Professor, last night I promised your services to a criminal gang which is going to steal something large. They'll need municipal equipment to pull off the job, a check of state road work plans, and for you to store the hot merchandise. Oh, and there will probably be hostages who need to be guarded for a while."

Arthur Mason glared at me quietly as the waiter came to ask if Carolyn would care to substitute a side dish for the potato-based pastries of which they had run out. Without glancing at the departing server he said plainly, "I'm going to hear you out because I think you're an OK fellow, on the right side of things I mean. But I'm going to be deciding right now if you're just plain crazy or not."

He picked up a fork and held it between both hands, just to have something to fiddle with. "Come on then, give me your pitch."

I folded my hands in front of me, elbows on the table, and tried to explain the plot without getting overly animated. "You know Carolyn has been inside Zelatoff, and she got a scoop. Well the scoop is that we know when another truck is going to Zelatoff, and we know where it is going to be 'disappeared'."

"Just so you can find out how they disappear?" he asked me accusingly.

"No. No, I really don't care," I insisted. "I want to get to the bottom of the whole thing. I'll bust up the plot if I can. Remember that someone is probably dead because of this business."

"Oh, now you think the death is related? Last week you wanted to keep a hundred feet away from that. If it is related, shouldn't it be a police matter?" The professor idly tapped the table with the fork handle as I spoke.

"It's still a long shot, and I've got nothing to give the cops to work with. You know as well as me that if they do start sniffing around Zelatoff about a murder everything will shut down and a mob of lawyers will get in the way."

I was pointing and gesturing now. "There's another reason I want to do it this way. I want to sell the load of material right back to Zelatoff. I think it's only fair that I get paid that much for my trouble."

The professor was quite sure then that I was insane. But he loved the idea too much himself to leave the asylum. I covered the general outline of the plan before appetizers were set before us.

He turned to Carolyn, "Did you have any idea what he was like when you signed on for this? You really know how to pick 'em," he added before she could answer.

"Oh, I think we share a certain level of motivation when it comes to... problems that sting personally. I knew from the first night Nick was going to figure this out." Carolyn sent a smile my direction and turned back to the professor. "I'm looking forward to seeing some 'normal' private investigator work, but this is a good case as it is."

"Normal?" I asked with a raised brow. "Don't expect anything to come at us that looks like any sort of 'normal.' People don't need to hire investigators when normal things happen." The line of conversation presumed that we would keep working together. I didn't have any objections to that idea.

I got back into the details with the professor. We would need a few road work signs from municipal stores. Since road improvements were pretty much on hold during the war he said he could pick those up without trouble.

We were going to set up a fake work site. We needed to know that there wasn't a real work site planned for anywhere close to our location. He said he knew where to call. Carolyn would call, posing as a someone planning a vacation and wanting to avoid delays.

I was unsure what he would say about storing a stolen heavy truck and its cargo. "Not a problem," he reassured me. "The fire department is short on men and engines right now. They reorganized and closed up two of the stations a while back. We can park it right where a ladder truck used to sit." He was sure it would not be noticed there.

By the time our dinners came I had broached the subject of the human beings we would probably snatch up. I said there should be two, one patsy and one actual gang member. I had no way to know how much of a fight either would put up.

We talked about the textbook ways to keep a confrontation from getting out of hand. Carolyn looked on, taking mental notes. I explained that rapidity-of-action and overwhelming force were the methods of my plan. The professor agreed that it was probably enough. I promised I wouldn't ask him to bury any bodies.

Eventually conversation drifted to the sort of small talk that normal people would have had at the beginning of the evening. I don't recall much else about the meal or the show. They tell me the music was good.

We parted ways and each had a short night. Sunday we would be busy making ready.

## -20- May 3rd (Monday), Arizona highways

Professor Arthur easily obtained the official items we would need. George Zografos didn't care to meet him face-to-face, but he sent August along to help, and to check out my side of the operation I'm sure. For his part George had what he promised loaded on a truck before sunset. I slept well Sunday night and was up early.

Monday morning we didn't meet in Tucson. We drove separately in three vehicles out toward the job site, by different routes. Shortly after noon I came into the entrance of an Apache-Sitgreaves National Forest campground. I stopped and got out to look at a forest map posted near the main gate. Stefano was already standing there. He saw me and walked back to his car without a word.

I waited a dozen seconds then got back into my own car. I pulled out of the park and drove over to the stretch of road I wanted to use. Stefano pulled out ten car lengths behind me. After another gap behind him would be a small commercial truck, the kind with toolboxes down both sides and a ladder rack on top.

170

(The rental would be added on to George's expense sheet.)

I had scouted ahead before picking up the rest of the crew. My chosen bit of gravel highway was near the end of a short straight, roughly northwest-bound. The forest was thick there, needly pines and evergreen shrubs kept back from the shoulder by infrequent maintenance. A narrow two-track around the next bend, grass growing tall over the last tread marks, afforded a place to stow the civilian vehicles while we worked.

We put on work clothes and put out the borrowed A-frame warning signs to close a short span of the west bound lane. Each man grabbed a tool and we began to dig. To look authentic, two-at-a-time we took turns leaning on a shovel watching the others work. But we kept moving on the shallow hole and had it dug in about two hours. The road bed was raised there so it was no trouble to simply toss the dirt and rocks off to one side.

In the whole time only two cars came along, by dumb luck at the same time and in opposite directions. A hastily improvised signal team got both vehicles through, well enough that an angry call to the state highway office was unlikely. I didn't think a call to complement our professional organization was going to happen either.

I stayed out of the way while the lumber and jacks were being placed. Everything was pre-cut but some last minute adjustment was needed, by application of a small hand saw to the two thickest posts. A few extra nails were called for after a first test run left August frowning more than usual.

Eventually, but well before dark, the plywood cover was placed for the last time and a layer of earth and gravel spread over it. Tools were put away, the truck hidden, and everyone found a comfortable hiding spot to sit out the coming wait. I was the only one who had thought to bring insect repellent so I left it with the others before I went to where I had to be.

I drove several dozen miles away from the setting sun, into the creeping front of the indigo night sky. The moon was supposed to be full that day, but it was to set at night, not to appear again until after seven a.m.

Eventually I found a good place to wait, a rural corner store closed for the day. I was suddenly nervous. I had every reason to be anxious, but up to that point I had been too busy to let myself feel it.

I went through a practiced routine of exercises to kill the butterflies and settle my mind. I smoked a cigarette too, but I would have done that anyway.

I thought about getting shot down by Angela Vickers in sixth grade. I thought about getting shot for real behind an underground casino in Newark. I thought about the current situation and decided everything that could be done to control my situation had been done. I was at peace. If things went badly it was just dumb luck. I might have said a prayer for good luck, but I didn't think the sort of quest I was on would make me Athena's favorite.

I wondered how they were getting along back in Tucson. The professor and Carolyn were readying a space for the expected guests. Arthur was sure enough about being able to use one of the idle fire stations that they were adding cots and padlocks to a storage locker there. It would be cozy if we took in three people, but I expected just two and hoped that the patsy on this gig would understand quickly that he'd been duped so we could cut him loose.

Sometime around two a.m. I saw the refraction of vehicle headlights in the store windows I had set myself behind. I started my engine and let it idle quietly as the truck approached. It turned out to be a medium size flatbed, faintly illuminated by the headlights of a car two hundred yards behind it.

This truck was an International D-series like the other one, but one size smaller. It had a solid green cab, whereas the first one was red. Details like this hadn't mattered to me when I took the escort job, but I was paying attention to everything this time.

I let both pass out of sight then turned on my alternate headlights, the smaller set, and pulled out behind them. They were just barely in sight when they turned onto the dirt highway through the national forest. I followed them in, keeping a distance that had me only intermittently in the mirrors of the chase car.

Following the established modus operandi, the truck stuck stubbornly to the 35 mile-per-hour limit. It took the majority of an hour to approach the trap we had set. Three miles out I made my move.

I increased speed incrementally, closing distance on the chase car without alarming the driver any sooner than necessary. I was going about fifty when I came to within a hundred feet of the other car. He had sped up a little, closing the gap to his charge, but had no reason to think I was anything other than another motorist who was tired of the crawling pace and wanted to get by.

I corrected him of that idea by switching back to my full power headlights and running up on him, surging by at speed in the oncoming lane. I glanced over briefly to see the driver working his controls, reaching down to flash his headlights repeatedly at the truck in front of him.

I started to overtake the truck, but it was accelerating. That was fine by me, as we expected the truck to be going fast, but it had to stay in its lane. I checked that my carbs were on maximum power and yawed open the throttle another controlled measure.

Then the truck went dark. Every light on it shut off in one click. I hesitated, swerving a little to the left to avoid the new unknown to my right. Catching a few edges lit by the chase car I got my bearings again and continued along beside the rushing flatbed.

I got up alongside the truck cab and could hear its engine working. We must have been doing almost sixty when I saw the marker we had placed on the left side of the road. I cheated to the left to make some space between my car and the ill-fated truck. We passed the marker and I braked hard.

The headlights of my car and the chase car badly lit the action. The truck nosed down suddenly, then leapt upward leaving a foot of air under the cab. The cab came down again just as the rear axle hit the initial dip. The entire frame of the truck settled into a storm of dust, suddenly dead-still and level with the ground.

The truck engine continued to turn, aggressively spinning the drive wheels, but the engine only made noise and the tires only churned the floating dust. Another vehicle was coming the other way, lights beaming through the dirt cloud. Voices and heavy footfalls approached from left and right. I was out of my car and running off to meet one of the voices to the left.

Just seconds later the chase car came to a stop thirty feet behind the truck. The hired security man got out, revolver in hand. He looked around quickly, then approached the back of the truck in a useless crouch.

"Hold it right there!" I called out as Stefano and I walked out from the close brush. The man turned, revolver level. I gave him a chance to size up the situation. He saw me with my 9 mm pistol aimed with both hands. He saw the starkly lit profile of Stefano behind me, bearing the unmistakable profile of a drum-fed Thompson sub-machine-gun. He didn't even know about George's mechanic coming up behind him with a pump shotgun when he lowered his revolver and stood up straight.

He was a young fellow, overdressed in a cheap suit. He had probably put up a sign as a private investigator just a month before. I laid it on thick.

"My name is 'you don't know.' Your name is 'I don't care.' Drop the gun for the man behind you to pick up and I'll tell you what happens next."

He started to turn suddenly, then had the smarts to stop and do it slowly, crouching down to set his standard .38 revolver two feet behind where he had stood. He looked up to see the mechanic, then turned to face me standing up again.

"Here's the deal. You've been duped, whether you want to believe it or not. That truck was going to disappear on you tonight, whether we took it or not. For now, you're coming along. You'll be cut loose when I say so. Got it?"

"Who the hell are you?" the young man asked indignantly. "I'll figure this thing out on my own just fine. Where did you say we were going?" He couldn't decide if he wanted to be mad or clever. I didn't have time or patience to deal with him that night. Stefano and the mechanic tied his hands and led him to their car.

I went to see how they had fared with whoever was in the truck cab. I approached the truck from behind, amused at the sight of its rear bumper set down into the dirt. I walked around the right side, off the road shoulder, looking into our trap with George who had a flashlight on it.

The pits had been just deep enough to leave a truck like this high-centered, frame on the ground, while its wheels spun. Earth ramps led into two separate pits, the second pit having a sheer far wall. Our wood framework was built to bridge over both pits, stout enough to carry any vehicle likely to come along that road.

But the frames had a built-in weakness. Each span was supported at the center by a cross-beam that rested on one of the large mechanic's jacks we had brought. Our mechanic tended the jacks all night, keeping them tight in case any cars did come by. Then when he saw me trying to pass the truck he released both jacks and got away from the pits.

My curiosity was hotter than ever as I got up past the cab of the truck. In front of the truck stood August and Smithy, either side of the kneeling solo driver of the truck. The driver was familiar to me. I finally connected that Harvey from the car dealership in Phoenix was "Slim" Hackett in my pictures from San Diego.

The man was sitting calmly, not presenting any hint of resistance. August explained, "It was easy to take this one. You should see the contraption he had on his face when we pulled him out of the truck." He pointed up toward the cab and I went to look.

On the passenger side of the bench seat sat a heavy canvas satchel, filled with a hard rectangular box shape. It was one of the large Army battery packs like Carolyn had seen.

Next to the battery was a contraption that was part gas mask, part binoculars, part blender. It clearly was meant to be strapped over one's head, covering the eyes. From there a metal housing took over, joining together multiple functional blocks. Protrusions on the bottom did resemble gas mask canisters, though this mask would leave the nose and mouth open to the air. In front of the wearer's eyes were two large circular lenses, almost eight inches forward. Another block attached to the top had transverse metal fins for cooling.

I felt the fins and found them still hot. A few minutes before they might have been painful to touch. The whole thing had an adjustable harness and a thick cable that plugged into the battery pack. The only controls appeared to be a toggle switch and a single knob on the right side.

I tentatively switched the device on, turned the knob both ways through its range, and switched it off again. It hadn't hummed or made any other external sign of function. I brought the unit up to my face and found the inside pitch black. I pulled on the harness and got the heavy device to sit on my face, with some discomfort at the weight. I switched it on again, while facing out the front of the truck cab.

I was immediately blinded by a tremendous blast of pale green light. The headlights of the two vehicles facing me became high power spotlights. The inside of the device in front of my face was flooded with painful brightness. I ripped off the machine, which lit up the whole truck cab. I found the switch and shut it off again.

Having some idea then what it was for, I took it with me out of the truck. I adjusted the one knob more carefully, switched the thing on again, and faced out into the dark desert as I tentatively brought it back up to my face.

The desert came alive like it was dawn. The image before me was monochrome, but detailed and deep. As far as the slightest light from our cars shone out a clear image came back to me. With some adjustment I could make out more distant hillsides lit only by the stars. The stars themselves came alive through the scope, some of the brighter dots being uncomfortable to look at as I adjusted the knob clockwise.

I took off the contraption and walked back to the truck. I had seen an extra pair of switches on the dash inside. In front of the truck I found another pair of headlamps, discreetly set inside the grill, like the extra lights on my own car. By naked eye a dim purple glow came from the nearest lamp. I stuck a hand out in front of it and with my other arm hefted the machine back up to my face. Through the eyepiece my hand shone brightly in front of the special lamp.

A voice behind me asked, "So what is that contraption?"

I shut it off, unbuckled the harness, and turned to answer George, "I'm not entirely sure, except that it's probably a military secret." I turned around and looked over the front of the truck again. "We need to clean up and get moving. I'll lock up this thing."

George was still curious but he agreed. Playing with the new toy would have to wait. Driving and hostage assignments were handed out. The jacks were used to get the big truck up and moving again. The mechanic and Smithy would stay behind to shovel dirt back into the hole, take up the road work signs, and get the small truck back to Tucson.

I didn't have any passenger with me. I would stop home for a moment then carry right on to Palm Springs and find a place to get some rest while the people from Zelatoff waited on their truck. Of course the truck wouldn't make it. I wanted to get there not long after they were sure it was missing.

-21- May 4<sup>th</sup> (Tuesday), Palm Springs, CA

On my first visit to the Zelatoff factory in Palm Springs I was hungry, tired, and nervous. This time around I was rested, sharp, and alert. It was early afternoon on a pleasant spring day. I was in no hurry. I kept my own pace, which I would for as long as I could keep control of my situation.

I walked slowly from the visitors' parking lot up a slight hill to the main office. The office block was an equal height extension of the main factory building, which ran off to the west, my left, so far it seemed sure to be built right into and through the mountain horizon. The entire building had clean lines, looking purpose-built in a modern way, but it was not a plain steel box.

Tall tinted windows were spaced between clusters of landscaping, in cycle with the blocks of the modular factory construction. Tying the whole thing together was a continuous red line, three quarters up the wall, not painted on but set into the wall panels, which ran directly into the iconic Zelatoff logo, 15 feet high on the top near corner of the building.

The entryway ahead of me was a giant sheet of glass running right to the roof. Set into the glass wall were two oversize glass doors. I pulled firmly on the right one only to stumble back as it swung with amazing ease. I let go of the door behind me and stopped to watch it glide as a thing of nature back through its arc to a dead silent stop where I had found it.

I turned back in toward the lobby to find myself in a spacious modern museum. The polished cut concrete floor looked almost wet and deep. A receptionist sat, looking completely incurious about her new visitor, at least 50 feet away in a tall room almost that wide. Small and large bits of the company's early efforts were mounted to the left, next to placards or signposts explaining each item. I chose to read over the materials along the right wall, which comprised a large print illustrated biography of Mister Penko Zlatkov.

Born in 1878 in Baltimore, Maryland, to an immigrant carpenter-turned-building supplies baron, Zlatkov took top marks in school, all while working every job in the family business. Always tinkering with whatever new technology was in the science magazines, he had three patents waiting for industrialization by the time he finally got the family inheritance out of trust.

If you own a compact "Microtube" radio, you know the rest. The American-ized name Zelatoff is in front of you every day, in your house, in your car, or even as you walk around if you were lucky enough to snag one of the pre-war "Townman" portable models. Zelatoff equipment was in every new TV studio, most science labs, thousands of industrial sites, and sold to common people in every town across the continent. Conspicuously absent from the list of major clients and retailers was the United States military.

The verbiage about the man and his company was definitely part of a home field program, but it was not boastful or jingoistic. As I strode across the hard floor toward the receptionist, I thought to myself that the ad men who wrote the copy were uncommonly tasteful.

The receptionist finally looked up at me when I crossed over on to the carpet that surrounded her area, my footsteps falling silent. She was an older lady, looking prim but not unpleasant, efficient without being terse. A perfect professional receptionist.

"Good afternoon. How may I help you?" She closed a thin black portfolio-style notepad and set down a pen on top of it. There was nothing else on her expansive desk but a faux leather bound calendar book and a plain telephone with only a few preset buttons on it.

"I'm sorry that this is something of a cold call, but I have something to offer that I can only think of this place as really being interested in." I had my hat in my left hand. My right hand curled over the edge of the raised front portion of the reception desk. I leaned in over the desk just a little.

She reached into a drawer to produce a small memo pad. "Very well, if you can tell me something about it, I'm sure I can get a message to the right department. Or did you have a letter prepared to leave?"

I stood up straight, pulled a folded slip of paper from my pocket, and handed it over. "That precise list of goods should be told to Nigel Thompson, in security. You'll find him very interested in hearing about it, the sooner the better. I'll wait." I added without further prompting, "My name is Nicolas Guyon."

I walked back to a short row of thinly padded chairs to the right of the reception desk. I turned to sit and found the receptionist still looking at me quizzically, the paper in her hand. She reached into a drawer to bring out another telephone as I got settled. Quiet words were said into the phone and an answer came back. She called another number, had another short conversation, and put the phone back away.

Four and a half minutes later Nigel Thompson himself came out of one of the two doors behind the reception area. "Nicolas Guyon," he appraised me from about fifteen feet away, "I understand you have some business to discuss."

"That's right. Are you the one who's going to talk about it, here?" I stood up, holding my hat.

"You can leave the hat here," he said, gesturing toward the reception desk. "We have to go upstairs."

I handed my hat to the receptionist, who placed it on a low table behind her. Mr. Thompson pointed me toward the door he had come out of. He followed a few feet behind me. I wasn't packing anything, but I think he was watching for bulges in my suit as I moved.

The door opened into a well-lit stairwell. Open frame stairs to my right, five feet wide with good thin

184

carpet on the tread plates, led up to a generous landing mid-way to the next floor. Turning around to take the next flight, I saw Mr. Thompson still holding good tactical position below me, to the outside where he had the longest vision around the turn. I also saw another younger man in a dark suit at the top of the stairs.

The younger man stepped back through the doorless opening at the top before I got there, as soon as Mr. Thompson started up the last steps behind me. I followed through into a wide carpeted hallway. Hardwood paneling low on the walls gave way to expensive textured wallpapers of muted solid colors. There were no light fixtures, but the very top edges of the walls glowed along their entire length.

Mr. Thompson entered the hallway behind me and gestured to the right as he said, "All the way to the end." I walked ahead as my two escorts laid back to either side behind me. Five feet from the only door in the end wall he said to hold up, and brushed close past me to get to the door himself.

With his hand on the knob, he turned back to tell me, "Mr. Zelatoff asked to speak with you personally. Since you dropped in unannounced, you may have to wait a bit." I simply nodded and the door was opened.

Zlatkov's outer office was small, considering the scale of everything else in the building so far. A modest desk with a phone like the receptionist's downstairs joined two waiting chairs and a small table between them to furnish the room. A carafe of water, two glasses, and some pre-wrapped crackers sat on the table. There was no secretary.

I told Mr. Thompson that I'd be fine waiting there. He pointed out the small restroom off to the left, in case I might need it, and left. He didn't bother to spell out for me that one or both of them would be waiting outside the office to keep track of me. I took the presumption as a professional courtesy.

I sat down and waited. There was nothing else to do but let my hand play. I was completely at the mercy of these men. I could only count on them to be smart – the one load of junk I had was a crumb to them, but they didn't know who else was involved or what we knew about their operation. That was the joker in my hand.

I expected that calls were being made, records checked, informants tapped, and probably my car was being searched. (I had left it unlocked to save me any damage if they didn't have a good jimmy man.) In this kind of game, they can keep drawing cards to build the best hand.

I waited twenty-two minutes. The four-foot-wide solid wood door at the back of the outer office opened fast. A short wide-shouldered man appeared just long enough to tell me, "Come in."

## -22- May 4th (Tuesday), Palm Springs, CA

I stepped without delay into the personal office of Mr. Penko Zlatkov, closing the heavy door easily behind me. Zlatkov moved without any hitch from his years to the desk. His gray textured suit was well cut. I said he was wide, but I don't mean fat. He was built of old brick.

The office was generous, made more spacious by the sparseness of its lightweight furnishings. Zlatkov's desk was open below the solid synthetic top. His only files would be in a low cabinet on the wall behind the desk. A small meeting table with tube frame chairs sat to my right.

Taking up a broader space on the left was a set of architectural models on dedicated stands. The factory complex we were in, at a scale making the model over six feet long, sat under glass. Next to it on an open table was a higher scale model of the company museum through which I had entered.

I spoke first, standing near the models as Zlatkov took a seat behind his desk. "Thank you for seeing me on such short notice, Mister Zlatkov." I attempted his real name the best I knew how.

He refined the statement, "Zero notice, actually, and that is somewhat distressing to a man like myself." He spoke with a hint of a Slavic accent, despite what the museum bio said about him being born and raised in the U.S.A.

"So I should gather from what I read in the lobby." I gestured toward the museum model. "My compliments to your ad men, by the way. Your biography was sublimely written."

"I wrote every word of that myself!" Zlatkov seemed truly flustered by me now. "Writing is easy when it's the truth." He quickly composed himself, set both hands apart on his desk, and bade me to proceed. "Now then, what did you come here to tell me?"

I walked closer to his desk and remained standing. "It's as simple as could be. I have, that is I came into possession of, something that once belonged to you. I should like to return it, and am here to discuss the terms for my services in the matter."

"Mister Guyon, you are a competent thief and a very unclever liar." Zlatkov sat back, hands on the arms of his chair. His rectangular face took on its more familiar pose representing a man who wills his own destiny. His slicked-back thinning dark hair only reinforced the long life experience he had at it.

"Sticking to what we both know, and know that the other knows," he explained, "you have a load of somewhat precious materials. I need the materials, but I can replace them at government controlled prices. And they are insured anyway, which is a condition of any new government contract. So why come to me when you could fence the material at a better rate than I would need to pay?"

I sat down and got comfortable before starting into my prepared answers. "Can you really get replacement materials? The production boards are supposed to have everything allocated by priority, and they claim it's all booked up at least a year in advance already. As for me, I could try to fence the lot, and while it's a small bucket to you, it's a lot for me to move around. I'm not that well connected in those sorts of things. Your company is a one-stop-shop for me to unload the whole heap."

Zlatkov admitted a slight grin. "Come now, Mister Guyon. You know very well how these things work. You have worked your way around ration boards to get what you need, and that trunk full of gas coupons you have is certainly counterfeit." He pulled open a thin drawer under his side of the desk, drawing out a gilded cigarette case. I took his offer of a hand-rolled smoke and lit it as he continued. Even up close his face looked shaven impeccably clean and smooth. Untamed dark eyebrows were the only distraction from the order of the old man's appearance. "Let us consider the one truck load a settled matter. You will sell it back to me, the price is a small detail." He tapped out the first ashes from his cigarette then sat back again. "Since you are here, we have more important things to talk about.

"It is no accident that you were chosen for that first little security detail," he continued. "You left a small legend behind in New Jersey. We have been looking for people we thought could be loyal, but with something of, shall we say, an entrepreneurial spirit." He took another long draw from his cigarette. "Our associates need to get jobs done, sometimes with less respect for larger authorities."

"As large as the federal government?" I asked without inflection.

"There is none larger, and none so useless!" Zlatkov gestured broadly, sat back for a moment, and continued. "Mister Guyon, I wasn't just born in this country, this country raised me. My mother bore me at the age of forty-two; I was the only one of us to survive the experience. My father also died that day, though it took him a long time to find his end at the bottom of a bottle." He pointed across the room to the museum model. "You won't read that part on any of those signs. After that I was on my own, with nothing but America itself to mother and discipline me."

Zlatkov was smiling at his reminiscing, his thoughts well past the distant loss of his parents that he hardly knew. "I do love this country. The fools who think they run it though... Let us agree that we can do better."

"Most of the time, I am inclined to agree," I confirmed.

"Most of the time?" Zlatkov pressed the point. "Do you maybe think this war being on gives them greater license? Come with me and we'll see about the rest of the time." He crushed out his half burned cigarette and waved me toward the door I'd come in.

I exited the office to find the young suit from earlier, leaning against the wall twenty feet away, arms crossed. He stood up straight and tensed for a moment, until he saw Zlatkov come out behind me. The younger man was dismissed and Zlatkov led me along himself. He moved with the slight aid of a polished black walking stick, I couldn't say if it was exotic hardwood or some more exotic synthetic.

The hallway had just a few unlabeled solid wood doors to either side, plus the open stairwell by which I had come. At the very end one small open area to the right had a secretary's desk, with secretary installed. Zlatkov traded familiar smiles with the young woman and opened the last door.

We stepped out onto a steel mezzanine overlooking the main factory floor, from fifteen or twenty feet above. There were few windows in the factory but it was uniformly well lit. Workers moved at an even pace among the stations. From above the organization of production was instantly recognizable. I had no idea what was being made, but it was clear where material went in, where the product was inspected between each operation, and who was responsible for approving each batch before it was packed for a truck.

The proud owner next to me let me take it in for a minute before jumping into his speech, which spared the usual details of a plant tour. Occasionally he gestured with the walking stick, or tapped it on the steel plate under our feet.

"What would they say about a place like this in New Jersey, Mister Guyon? Would they think it even possible?"

I watched a fork lift deftly pick up an empty wire crate and turn in one motion to zip down a center aisle. It traveled that straight line so far it nearly disappeared into a perspective well. "I don't know many industrialists to ask, but a place this size would get the attention of a wagon load of county clerks looking for the right permits to be paid up."

Zlatko chuckled warmly. "You're a step ahead of me, Nicolas!" He literally looked to the east as he talked about them. "Those people in the east, who don't know anything outside of their little world, from Baltimore to Boston, they still think of the west as a colony. All those famous railroads they built, they set them up to be one-way streets, hauling loads of ore and timber and cattle to where the big cities could make anything useful out of them. If a Navajo blanket got thrown in as a gift to someone's niece, fine, but otherwise nobody dreamed of finished goods coming out of this territory."

He turned back to gaze down into his factory. "Do you know what they made here before I came?" I shook my head at the rhetorical question. "Wagon wheels. Wooden wagon wheels, things for donkey carts like some of the old Mexican farmers still use. Nobody was making even cheap window glass west of Texas, now we make the highest grades in the world, thinner than ever thought possible, just as one part of our tubes."

"Those who pay a little attention to the west, they talk about Henry Kaiser's cement plants as big industry making a stake out here. But, after the government is tired of building its big dams, who is going to be buying the concrete? *Me*, that's who."

He swept his arm across our view of the plant. "This is the fifth factory we've built, each larger than the last. All are still in operation, except the first which you may know is now probably the top R&D facility in business."

"Mister Guyon, normally I let Mister Thompson do his own recruiting for the sort of work he gets done for me." Zlatkov was facing me directly now. My body was still square to the rail, my face turned only partly toward the shorter man. "It was he who hired you in the first place. Do you know why I chose to see you personally today?"

"I was hoping you'd get to that, actually. I suppose you want me to work for you, but not just for the cash. So what's the pitch?" I fished out my pack of cigarettes, for something to do with my hands while I entertained my host.

The pitch came. "This war will be over sooner or later, and I think sooner. You've heard politicians talk about 'winning the peace' as well, but of course they mean ensuring their party or union or pet industry comes out on top in their new plan for the world. Nicolas, I'm actually afraid, afraid of what this monster we've built will do. Its hunger may not slake once there is no war to feed it the power it craves."

He thrust the knob of his stick toward me to emphasize his question, "Do you think the autocrats who will claim to have won the war and remade the world will simply accept their medals and go home? No, I think most of them would just as soon go on running things as they see fit, with other people's money and sweat, of course."

He moved around me to continue down the catwalk. "Walk with me as we talk." I followed him to the far end and through another door, this one windowless and metal clad. The cramped room we entered wasn't particularly small, but it was heaped up with jumbles of electrical gear, boards packed with tubes, and what might be oversize light bulbs with flattened tops. Some of the material was on counters or tables. Piles of loose parts climbed five feet up the wall in two corners. The larger bits sat out on the floor. It was the darkest room in the building so far.

I recognized some of the larger parts. "It looks like you're ready to open a television repair shop, but I don't think you'd get much business. I think you've bought up half the sets in the world."

With a dry smile Zlatkov admitted, "Yes, it is a small market. There might be 50,000 sets out there, all of them hopelessly crude. Our new models will be much more compact, of course. It's one of the jobs my team has been working on. But the sets aren't what we're working on here. This is what we tore out of this facility just months ago. Go on to the next room."

194

I stepped around and over multiple electrical cadavers and their dusty guts to reach the next door. The adjoining room was a stark contrast. Neat, open, and sparsely populated with equipment, the only disorder came from two uniformed technicians who turned to observe the new visitors. On seeing Zlatkov they turned back to their console.

In front of them, to our left, was a wall of television screens, two dozen at least, about a foot wide apiece. Each was flatter and had a sharper looking image than any set I'd seen in a New York shop window. Against the far wall was a larger screen, set into an open frame which exposed an improvised assemblage of electrical parts. The image on that screen was in vibrant color. I recognized the scene as being the mountains just west of the factory. The sun was settling in between the taller peaks just then, painting some hillsides in rich golden tones and pushing the near slopes into dark contrast. It all came through in surreal clarity.

I looked back at the wall of smaller black and white screens and realized that they too were images from around the factory, inside and out. "Pretty slick setup, but can you get in the Yankees game?"

"Nicolas, again you are getting ahead of me. These are test images, from local cameras, but it is the programming we are working on here, or rather how it gets to the viewers. Television broadcasting has been what they like to call the 'wild west' up to now. But things are about to change. I was involved in some of the discussions in Washington, but I quit when I saw that the mind of the bureaucrats was already made up.

"A broadcast television signal is expensive, in terms of what the engineers call 'bandwidth.' They want to dole out frequencies under license, and are only going to give enough for a city to have three, maybe four, broadcasters. They told me it's "plenty," and are dead sure of themselves, with no idea of the potential here."

He shook a finger at the wall of screens. "Can you imagine it, Nicolas, if there were only three things allowed to be sold at a newsstand, *by law*, where publishers had to beg for a license and swear to some vague code? People wouldn't stand for it, or at least they shouldn't. Yet the existing syndicates are already being handed licenses in bulk, divvying up the country amongst themselves."

I shook my head gently, never taking my gaze away from the impressive visual display. "Aren't you the one getting ahead of yourself now? I don't see how it's all that bad, or that we won't figure things out differently later."

"But this is exactly how it already is in other countries – including the ones we fight now!" Zlatkov had both hands on his walking stick, which he struck on the hard tile floor for emphasis. "Yes, I am getting ahead of things, and that is exactly the point! Look here."

He opened a door in the far right corner of the room. It wasn't much more than a long equipment closet, which wrapped halfway around the room we had been in, with access to the rear of all the television monitors. Zlatkov reached to the far wall of the working space to lift up a slack loop of a wire which entered through the wall and then was tacked along it to feed a stack of equipment near the cluster of monitors.

"Everything you saw in the other room, it comes through this wire. Above us this wire, this copper wire, is coiled through almost five miles of length. With the right equipment on both ends, which we have developed, we can put not three, but thirty or even three hundred signals through one wire. Do you see what this means?"

I stared at the proud man a long second before answering. "Well, I suppose it would be a lot easier to sell ad time to a local boot shop if you had a station showing all western movies."

Zlatkov stared at me curiously for a moment then his face opened up into an earnest open mouth smile. "Again you make the next connection, Nicolas! Yes, a scheme like this can pay for itself quite easily. But we must be ready when the time comes, ready to show the world how it can work. We will have to get this wire out to every building in a major city, at once. We can't wait for some post-war committee to dole out material to us. The system has to be demonstrated at full commercial scale right from the start."

"So, Mister Guyon, we are back to our original conversation. We need to have material stockpiled to pull this off when the time comes. Now that you understand the need, you can make arrangements with Mister Thompson to return the missing copper."

"And the truck," I added.

"No, you can keep the truck. Just please remember that the 'Night Eye' binoculars, as we call them, are a military secret." Zlatkov was already walking back through the television shop. "I will make sure that Mister Thompson knows that you are selected for the most important assignments coming up. Of course he will also offer above market rates for the copper and for your professional services."

"I'll think about it."

"Think about which?" Zlatkov stopped in the middle of the piles of TV parts. "Nicolas, I'm sure that you are a careful man, but I've laid it out for you quite plainly. We have come together at a point of mutual opportunity."

"I'll think about both, the load of copper and about coming to work for you." I crushed out my cigarette against the top of an old wooden console, then flicked the butt into a pile of wires in the near corner."

"Mister Guyon, you distress me. You have me at some disadvantage after what I have told you. I trust your discretion, but know that I can't wait for very long on your answer."

Zlatkov continued onto the factory catwalk. Mr. Thompson was there to meet us, by coincidence or unseen summons. We reentered the office block and Zlatkov continued onward to his office without another word. I was escorted by his head of security all the way out to my car.

## -23- May 4th (Tuesday), Palm Springs, CA

I got in my car and was not surprised to see the deep-faced man sitting next to me.

"Hello, Nick. My name is Jack." He pronounced the hard "J" with excessive emphasis, like it was something he had to remind himself to do. Otherwise he spoke American English with a neutral accent.

I had my keys in my hand and was reaching for the ignition switch out of mechanical habit. "Your car will not start until I let it," he told me. He pulled out a small switch box with a wire antenna sticking out of it. "We need to talk for a minute."

I put the key in and let the ring hang from the switch. I turned to face him.

Sitting down "Jack" was six inches shorter than me. I knew he was on the short side, but he must have been all legs, too. His long arcing nose sat in odd upside-down symmetry with his cheeks, each gaunt and drawn out but capped with a firm round top. His bony brow had probably looked wrinkled since he was three years old. A high hairline was parted on the left, straight dark brown hair running a little longer than the current style to either side.

He came there to talk. I sat back and let him talk. "I trust you had an informative discussion inside?" I nodded yes. "Good. I do not know the details of what you might have been offered. I do not want to know. I am instructed to make sure you understand all the parameters of our offer."

I put my left forearm on the steering wheel and turned my body more toward him.

He continued. "The vehicle you hijacked is one of two we have set up for our work. The load coming this time next week is to arrive normally, as is the one soon after that. But then we must have the vehicle working for us again."

I told him to continue as I rolled down a window and got out a cigarette. I did not offer him one. I laid my idle arm back on the wheel.

"You think this is too much for me to tell you, that I am a fool, yes?" I remained blank. "Let me also tell you that we know your lady friend left here and returned to Tucson by bus."

My hand gripped the steering wheel tightly. It took mental effort not to look at my own tell, relax my grip, and hope he hadn't noticed.

"The situation is very simple. The deadline is real, as are the consequences. If we find the vehicle, or the girl, before you accept our offer, you will have lost leverage and gained a powerful enemy."

I let him wait as I took a long drag of smoke and blew it up into the air above us. "Sounds like a fair game to me."

He smiled, a toothy sweeping smile. "Also, I shouldn't need to tell you, but you also have some equipment of sensitive military nature. If it is not accounted for it is the FBI you will be talking to."

I looked square at him to ask, "Was it the FBI that Sam Windham had trouble with?"

The smile was gone. Jack fingered the radio switch absentmindedly. "Mister Windham made an enemy," is all he would say about that.

Jack reached into his lightweight tweed jacket. He pulled out one of my ignition wires and tossed it in my lap. "There is no device installed on your car." He held up the switch box again, "This is a handy prop, but the simple solution is usually best."

Without another word he exited and got in his own car, in the adjacent space. He pulled away and left me to repair my vehicle. I glanced just once up at the factory building, sure that cameras were watching me replace the wire.

I watched for a tail as I drove back to Tucson, turning and stopping and doubling back often. There was no tail, which was oddly unsettling.

At the first opportunity inside Arizona I stopped to make change and use a pay phone. I tried for Arthur Mason at home, at the gun club, and even bothered an

El Con manager to look for him. I gave up and went into the next town.

What passes for a downtown in Quartzsite, Arizona, was big enough to have a small Western Union office. I sent a telegram, priority delivery in person, giving them several addresses to try.

**MOVE C'YN, +2, SD. HAVE MALICK
SUGGEST PLACE. USE DISCREET CREW**

I wanted Carolyn and her children moved out of Tucson, all the way to San Diego, immediately.

## -24- May 4th (Tuesday), Tucson, AZ

The remaining few hours' drive was quiet. Even my thoughts were still. Certainly I had problems, but they were few in number and acutely focused.

I had poked the bear. The bear growled. That's the way it goes.

I still had no tail. They probably had my address in Tucson. It wasn't advertised, but I'd been getting mail there for months. Someone would probably try to pick me up there and see where I went around town.

Still I didn't dare drive by Carolyn's place or the fire station to check on the arrangements at either. I drove straight home.

A message was waiting for me, saying Ross Malick had called. That bothered me. I didn't have any other mail, which was unhelpful but unsurprising.

It was getting late, but I didn't know what sort of hours Malick kept. I decided to try him back, but not from my motel phone. I washed my face and found my shoulder holster. It was too hot for my jacket, but the world had gotten too dangerous to go out with just a little revolver in my pocket.

I walked across the street and up to the diner where I was familiar. There was a pay phone there, but it was on a pole outside. I asked the hostess if I could use their office phone for some confidential business.

"Ooh, Nick, something exciting finally come up? You going to tell me about it later?" She knew something of my business, the parts I'd told her for her amusement. I assured her that all the dirt would be planted in her ear as soon as it could be told.

I closed the office door in front of the curious woman and got connected to Ross Malick's office. He was working late, "As usual," he said. "It's a circus over here, with the Army and Navy and city and county police all tripping over each other, plus double the number of people from two years ago. A lot of things fall between the cracks for us privateers."

"Say," he continued, "if you ever want a piece of the action, I've got work to spare."

"There are plenty of crooks in Tucson," I assured him (I had four of them working for me, after all). "I just need to find clients willing to pay to meet them."

I changed to a less friendly tone. "So what's the idea of calling me direct?"

"Right, sorry chum," he said contritely. "Actually, I called you and left a message before the other fellow called me about the... the other problem." His voice quieted a little, "Can we talk about that where you are now?"

"Yes, we can," I assured him. "But at this point I'd rather not know the details of the final solution."

"I understand." He was back to a relaxed tone. "Well, it will take a couple days but I told your man I can get it done."

My face tightened at that timing. Carolyn might not have a couple days. But I couldn't expect lodging in San Diego to come that easily. "That will have to do," I said through a grimace. "So what was it you called about in the first place?"

Papers shuffled on the other end of the phone. "Your pal Sam Windham; I got the scoop on his murder."

I hmm'ed for him to continue. The murder part wasn't news any more.

"His car's brake lines had been cut, rear then front in sequence. It happened by remote control, based on the radio receivers they found, tied to small charges on the tubes. It was a real neat job. Might have been mistaken for original equipment on the car if it had fallen all the way down and been smashed up more."

"That's exactly what I needed to hear," I enthused. It certainly fit a going hypothesis. "Was it hard to get the info?"

"You kidding? The deputies think it's a cool story, real whiz-bang spy stuff. They're all talking about it. Actually, on the spy angle the military and FBI are having a look at it. Now, what I had to ask more roundabout-ish were the other details."

"Oh? Like what?" I was reaching for a scrap of paper in the restaurant office and looking for a pen.

"The electrical hardware was all custom, not a part number or brand logo on any piece, the case, coils, anything."

I started to replace the torn-off bottom third of an invoice for dinner rolls, then balled it up and tossed it in the trash can.

"OK, thanks again," I offered. "Nothing to follow up on there, but it still fits a theory. Anything else?"

There was nothing else of interest. I let Malick go and pulled a slip of paper out of my jacket. I dialed the number to the closed-down fire station (why they still paid for a line there was a matter for the county administrators).

After seven rings Arthur Mason answered, "Hellow?" in a lousy falsetto that I saw straight through.

"Can it, Professor, it's Nick."

"I'm sorry," he continued in the awful 'housewife' voice, "You have reached the Nelson residence. Would you like to speak to the Admiral?"

"Aw geeze," I sighed. "Do I really deserve..."

"Yes, you deserve it!" he exclaimed, still amicably. "Every time I've said 'yes' to you you've upped the ante, when I didn't even know I was playing a hand. So, what, now you're calling to tell me what a bad day you've had?"

I took my lumps from him meekly and explained about the threat against Carolyn and that I'd spoken to Malick.

"Sure, Carolyn is right here. Do you want to speak to her?"

"No, wait!" I tried to keep Arthur on the line. "I really don't want right now to..."

"You!" I heard, in a tone of voice I would have heard from my mother if I had just shaved the neighbor's dog. "You want to tell me why I have to explain to two little children why mommy has two men locked up in a cage?"

I put together that Arthur had pulled them out of the apartment right away on getting my telegram and they were all hiding at the fire station. It wasn't quite what I meant, but I couldn't say it was wrong.

I really was curious about how she had explained that one to the kids, but parenting tips would have to wait. I explained that Zelatoff had linked us and saw her leave for Tucson, if not followed her further. I added confirmation that someone had been killed for being mixed up in this business.

She was silent for a moment. "So they would really kill people over this copper thing?"

"That's the way it goes, no matter how big or small the crimes. Once you're in on something shady, there's no easy way out if things go south, or if someone steps out of line. I've tried to offer them a way out here, but they may be the sort who think it's safer to just 'clean up' the whole loose end."

"In for a penny, in for a pound," she quoted the old idiom. "It's not really news to me, but," she asked more softly, "do we really have to go all the way to San Diego?"

"Honestly it's just the first place that came to mind," I admitted. "But it's a place we both know a little now. Plus, I do have work for you there."

"Oh, Nick, I... I'll get it done. You know that."

"I know you have to get the children settled in first. Don't worry, we have a few days. I don't even know yet exactly what you'll need to do. It depends on what else I learn this week." I segued, "So, how are our guests behaving?"

She paused a second, to look toward them I supposed, "It's pretty quiet now. The young detective, Joseph, was talking up a storm, complaining and threatening and trying to interrogate me and Arthur and the other fellow."

"Is he any good at it?" I asked.

"Nick, he's terrible. He couldn't get an address out of a phone book."

I grinned. "How about the other fellow?"

"Harvey doesn't say much. He's been very patient. He explained that he knows he can't talk to the authorities or he'd have to answer for the original scheme with the trucks. I think he trusts us, in an odd way."

"Honor among thieves," I idiomized the notion. "It works as long as everyone has dirt on the others. We can't very well turn him in without answering for locking up two men for a week."

"Right. But Harvey did finally speak up, just to shut up Joseph. Harvey confirmed that he really had been duped, that he was only along as an independent witness to sign off on whatever story Zelatoff prepared. Joseph might be coming around after that lecture. Nick, will it really be a week?"

"Let him think it will be two," I added. "Mention that we need the other truck. Then we won't need him and can send him home."

She said she could sell that. I asked to get the professor back on the phone. I asked him if he agreed with Carolyn's assessment, that the P.I. Joseph was more or less on our side and that Harvey was square with his situation.

He figured she was about right. Plus, we didn't have the man power to keep guarding the prisoners. Stefano was due to babysit them at night, but soon he was going to help move Carolyn. And George hadn't promised me use of his crew indefinitely.

I said to hire young Joseph to escort Harvey on an express bus to St. Louis. From there we would cut Harvey loose with twenty dollars' pocket money.

The professor was a little incredulous, "Do you really think Harvey will sit quietly and be escorted halfway across the country by this kid?"

"Of course not," I confirmed with him. "He'll jump ship and slip away at the first pit stop. But then we'll probably never hear from either of them again. Harvey will report back to Nigel, but only what he knows. Does he know where he is?"

"There isn't much equipment left here, but he's probably figured out it's a fire station. And he'll know he's leaving Tucson when we put him on a bus."

"Right. We're going to have to move the truck. When I figure out where to you'll be the second to know."

I had used up the hospitality, and impatient curiosity, of my restaurant host. A short knock on the door was followed immediately by a hand trying the locked door knob. I finished with the professor and hung up.

I opened the inward swinging office door and the familiar waitress nearly fell in with it. I held out a couple dollar bills for the long-distance call and she took the cash sheepishly. It dawned on her that she would have to either give the money to the owners and tell them she'd let a customer alone in their office, or say nothing and explain it later if a pricey call was noticed on the bill, logged during her shift. Doing me favors was never easy.

I got back to my place and was soon in bed. I was hungry, sore, and tired. I had been too distracted to eat when food was right in front of me. I was too distracted then to sleep with a good bed immediately under me.

So far as I could tell I still had control of the game, the 'offensive impetus' an overwrought sports writer might call it. But the opponent had just forced the tempo. Risks had leapt in scale and quick action was demanded to tame them and stay in the lead.

I considered the members of the opposition, their actions and what I estimated of their personalities. They had invested time and personal commitment to a certain plan, and it had started out well for them. If they were like any normal sort of people, they would stubbornly stick to what they had been doing.

I had a vision, a clear and simple vision. The vision was red. I slept well.

-24- May 5<sup>th</sup> (Wednesday), Tucson, AZ

I woke up peacefully, refreshed and ready for action. The only trouble was my presumption that I was being watched and would be followed. I would be a prisoner in my own home until I did something about that.

I got fully dressed like I was ready to go out for the day. I made a show of putting gear back in my car, including my guns. An awkward bundle, wrapped in a motel pillowcase and paired with a heavy satchel battery, went into the front of the car in the passenger seat.

I locked up the car and strolled out toward the road-facing motel office. I moved slowly, thumbing through my wallet as my eyes scanned my surroundings. I had never taken the time to memorize the details of my environment, but I hoped I might get lucky and pick up some obvious change.

I got lucky right away. The men sent to tail me had been fortunate to find vacant just the right cottage in the same compound. It was on the side of the main drive, close behind the front office building and with line-of-sight around the turn to my front door. The plain Chevy sedan in front of their room had new tires and a California plate, which would certainly trace back to a rental company. A man in a comfortable shirt sat reading a newspaper in the front seat.

I continued to the office, walking in the side door of the glass-walled lobby as always. As I opened the door I heard two short beeps from the motel parking lot. "Good morning, Nick," greeted the day manager. I bantered with him for a moment then asked if I could exit out the back door.

He seemed puzzled but not curious enough to question me. He showed me through the back office and laundry and unbolted the solid door for me. I came outside again and the suspect car was out of view. I crept up the side of the first residential cottage and peeked around the corner.

The car had a second passenger now, and its engine was idling. The car had no mirror on the passenger side so I walked up through the driver's blind spot until I was next to the rear fender. I gave the sheet metal two hard knocks then walked to the front of the car, getting a good look at the two men as I gave them a friendly wave.

The passenger waved back weakly after a pause. His partner went back to reading the paper. I walked casually back to my place. The two twenty-something men were probably fresh hires, or from very deep in the dugout of Nigel Thompson's gangster team.

They knew they were burned, which would make life easier for all of us. From then on they could stick to me like pine tar without worry. My mind would be at ease about them until they disappeared, which would mean someone better was sent to replace them. I hoped that would be a least a few days away.

I double-checked that my car was locked. I reassured myself that the men sent to follow me probably didn't have an assignment to break into my things, or the skills to do it neatly. I hadn't left anything useful to them anyway. I went to get an overdue and oversize breakfast.

I lingered over the meal, flipping aimlessly through a couple sections of a newspaper. Eventually I was done making my minders wait on me and got on with my day. I walked back to my car, tossed my jacket in the back, and headed north to the university.

I had to park a block away from the library on the mid-morning of a school day. I waited a moment to make sure the tail car got a spot in the same lot. I went over to the library and one of the men followed me.

Back in the reference section a couple two-day-old San Diego newspapers had no further news about Sam Windham. I didn't expect they would, but if some reporter had landed a scoop the details of the crime would make a titillating story. Word like that getting out would make Zelatoff skittish and might derail my plans.

Just for fun I circled through the library stacks, and up and down a floor, and lost my tail. He found me again in the outer lobby, buttoned up in one of the private telephone booths there.

I rang George Zografos at the number he'd given me. I didn't know where that was, but he was there, and he wasn't happy. Stefano had passed on to him that things had gotten messy. I did the best I could to put him at ease.

I explained that Zelatoff was willing to deal, but was putting pressure on us just to be cheap about it. I was sure they'd come around, but if he could start looking for other buyers of the copper that might give us better leverage to get a good price. It made sense to him in those dollars-and-cents terms.

In the mean time I had a plan to stash the load, then move and disguise the truck. I didn't tell him the part of the plan where we give the truck right back to Zelatoff.

The call done, I exited the phone booth, smiled at my shadow, and led the way back to our motel. This time there was mail waiting for me.

I locked my room, drew the blinds tight, and sat at the desk with my haul of new mail. All at once I had the written report from Kramer & Hodges in San Diego, the promised police records from New Jersey, a fresh bank statement, and a postcard from a new pop-up trade school promising certificates in welding, accounting, and culinary arts.

I reviewed the folders, pulled out the most important papers, and put together a portfolio on the case.

I wrote out detailed instructions for Carolyn. She would start by delivering new instructions to Kramer & Hodges. They said Zelatoff's law firm had pursued a lot of cases involving government contracts. I wanted them to find a name among the top Army buyers for Zelatoff.

I wrote three copies of a letter of introduction for Carolyn, adding Arthur Mason, Tucson P.D., retired, as a reference. She was going to walk into the offices of some self-important people who might not take seriously a pretty young lady. I made the portfolio as

216

concise and direct as I could. I knew that whoever she saw, Miss Carolyn Barnes would not take no for an answer.

Satisfied with the results, based on what I had to work with, I picked up the phone. I got professor Arthur at the fire station. I was quick, "I can't talk here. Have Carolyn meet me where Anne met me, at dawn on Friday." He acknowledged and we hung up.

There was nothing else to do for the day. I left my windows covered, not even peeking out at my personal surveillance team. I would rest and let them fret over what I was doing, if there was a back door or window to watch (there wasn't), and when I might move again.

I read a lousy novel to pass the time. The hero had photographic memory, perfect aim, and beguiling charm. It made for easy reading, and for the writer an easy solution to any problem in the plot.

I turned on the radio while I scrounged up food to improvise a supper. The newsman reminded listeners of the first anniversary of the battle of the Coral Sea, where Japanese armed forces were stopped for the first time in living memory.

Current news included failure of a bill in congress to cancel last year's income tax and switch to collecting tax on every pay check. The government said it was better for everyone, especially the government, but some folks couldn't stomach the idea that a lucky few would get a lucky break.

The news also announced that all American coal mines were under official government control. The coal strike was a month old then. The commentator had license enough to note that flying a national flag over each mine wouldn't by itself levitate any coal up through the shafts.

Night came. I fell asleep reading. Thursday came and it was a repeat of Wednesday.

I led my minders to the library, which again had no important news for me. I decided to run some routine errands. I made my minders wait while I went through the chore of counting out ration stamps for groceries.

The grocer reminded me that the allowance for coffee had been reduced and he stood firm on the limit. I took my haul out to the car and loaded the items in so the men tailing me could see the perishable items.

I stopped downtown to get postage stamps and envelopes. From there I drove around idly, enjoying a break in the hot weather. We paused to look at planes taking off and landing at the busy main air base.

I didn't even toy with my tail. I stayed on main roads and took an easy meandering route around town.

Early in the afternoon I pulled back into the motel, stopping at the office to pick up more mail. The shadow car paused in the street for a moment before they decided it was OK to pull in and park by their own door ahead of me.

My only mail was a single letter-size envelope, stuffed thick and covered with marks from several postal agencies. I moved my car to my door, unloaded the day's take, and sat down with the letter. It was from Ottawa, Ontario, Canada.

Four sheets of paper were tri-folded around two small photographic prints. The last three sheets were copies of official government files. The front page was a letter written in a flowing and precise longhand.

*Hello, Nicolas.*

*I trust this letter finds you in good health. I know that it comes to you while you pursue important business. It is lucky that you found me, as I should be retired by now, and agreed to stay on only until this war is over.*

*I have passed your name to my lieutenants here. They will know to lend you any assistance in the future in matters of mutual interest. They have already heard stories of your father, who I know was missed by both departments after his passing.*

*The man you inquired about is known to us. Jacques Tourel was active in Quebec and Ontario during your prohibition era. (Some think the Canadians sat back and took in tax revenue as our distilleries rushed the border, but you know we kept a close eye on them and struggled to keep the violent element at bay.)*

*M. Tourel worked for several distributors near the border. His role was never clear and he never stayed with one company for very long. We thought he was a sort of 'problem solver'. The pages you have now profile two of his former associates whose automobiles were sabotaged to fatal effect near the end of Tourel's tenure with a company. He was never implicated personally, but as you see we kept a file.*

*We would be interested in knowing what Tourel has been up to. A contact is provided for you, or for a local police office should they be involved in your case.*

*Good luck on your current and future endeavors. Please be safe.*

> *Col. M. Montgomery*
> *RCMP*

I immediately put the whole letter in the packet for Carolyn. I thought to pull out the hand-written part and write out a copy to send instead. I also added to Carolyn's instructions. She was to take Ross Malick along to the county sheriff, and be ready to talk to the FBI about everything.

My work for the day was done. That afternoon I made an effort to keep my minders at ease. I opened the curtains, took things in and out of the car, and was generally easy to observe doing a lot of nothing. I wanted these guys to stick around a while longer and not call for backup if they hadn't already.

I had to get up early so I made final preparations and went to bed. I wanted to check if the Army battery pack I had was still charged, but it had no gauge and I had no instrument to do the job. I had to hope it worked long enough to do one more gig.

My alarm went off before 4 am. I was confused and unhappy at first then remembered what I had to do and woke up sharply. I turned on lights which could be seen from outside. I showered and dressed. I had time to make myself a small breakfast, enjoying the fresh eggs, milk, and juice I had picked up the day before.

I stepped outside and buttoned up my suit jacket. It would warm up quickly once the sun was out, but the cooler weather of the day before left behind night air that was bracing.

I pulled out about quarter to five. I had given my friends plenty of notice and they were ready to get on the road right behind me.

I went northwest out of Tucson, out into the desert and away from any street lights. I kept a steady 50 miles per hour on the mostly flat open roads. I could have been going to Phoenix or back to Palm Springs but I was off the main highway, sticking to what paved secondary roads paralleled it.

The men following me had probably come with a full gas tank and kept it topped off. I could simply out last them in the desert with my deep tanks, but I didn't have that kind of time.

I didn't know the roads well. I only had looked at them on maps the day before. We were approaching a sequence of turns through some low hills before an open crossroads.

I fished the secret headgear out of its pillowcase cover. I hoisted the heavy machine over my head while trying to keep steady in my lane.

I upped my speed considerably approaching the first turn. The tires complained in chorus as they found the apex. I set up my overweight coupe for the next turn as my left hand found the headlight switch. The steering wheel pushed back almost too much for my right hand as I stole a glance in the dark rear view mirror.

There was a short straight before the last turn. I steadied the wheel and killed all the lights on my car. I let the contraption down the rest of the way onto my face and scrambled to find the on switch.

The machine took a nervous few seconds to warm up, but then I had a narrow but crystal-clear view of the oncoming road, lit only by ancient stars. (The moon would not rise until well after the sun that day.)

The turn came and I steered into it easily. At the last instant before rounding the curve I was blinded by the headlights of the following car, blasting at me at close range from my own mirrors. I smacked at the center mirror, partly negating the problem I should have anticipated.

I came out of the turn near wide open throttle. I backed off some and let the next intersection come to me. I hadn't had a chance to cancel the brake lights on my Lincoln so I would have to negotiate the turn with the hand brake.

With two hundred feet to go I pulled hard on the lever. A hundred feet later I pulled harder. It didn't have nearly the needed effect. I forced the turn anyway. Hard right steering and a little throttle brought the back end around. The hearty Lincoln skidded across all of the adjoining road's pavement before the rear wheels caught and pushed the car desperately to the right.

In the daylight the cloud of tire smoke would have been obvious. On that night I watched the chase car drive by it at speed. The Chevy's tail lights continued on toward the horizon as I carried on down dark narrow side roads. The pavement gave way to rough gravel. I took my time circling back around into northern Tucson.

Within ten minutes my neck was fatigued from supporting the machine in front of my face. I reached up to take it off and was nearly burned by the hot cooling fins on its top. I stopped so I could switch it off and take it off with both hands. I set it on the passenger seat with the battery pack, which itself was getting warm.

The lines of Sentinel Peak were graced by the slightest pre-dawn light as I approached the park entrance. I drove up to the summit and waited in the parking lot for true sunrise. At first light over the distant mountains I walked down to the city overlook. It was free of any tourist photographers that morning.

I thumbed through the folder I was carrying for a few minutes before a car came around behind my right. Mike Minervini, Smithy, was driving a plain four door car with three passengers. He stopped the car on the narrow drive and got out with Carolyn.

She approached me first. "Today's moving day. We're going straight from here to San Diego." She looked back toward the car. I looked with her and finally had a chance to see her children.

A precious little girl, I don't have a better phrase for her as she was cast perfectly into that common expression, stared out the near window at the vista over the city. The scene looked right back at her, painting her round face and curling fair hair with diffuse golden warmth.

A serious young man sat in the far side of the back seat. His passive stare fixed unwaveringly on me. His stare judged me and sized up my stature and honor next to his mother. I knew his only thoughts were of candy and toy soldiers, but I felt small.

I looked at the back of the car. It occurred to me that every last possession they had was packed into the modest trunk.

Smithy spoke up. "Everything's all set. We're gonna meet that Malick guy and they'll be all moved in today."

I addressed him directly, "Listen to me, Mike. This is serious. People are looking for them, for her. You might be followed. Carolyn knows how to lose them. She's in charge, no questions. You get that?"

"Aw, come on Nick, it's not like I don't..." he sized up my mood and decided to shelve the protest. "Yeah, yeah I got it. Whatever she says. I'll get 'em there, you don't worry about it."

I handed the folder to Carolyn and told her to read the instructions later. I didn't need to go over her itinerary in front of one of George's guys. She picked up on the issue and put the file in one of the bags in the trunk.

I encouraged Smithy to make good time getting to San Diego. "They've still got to get moved in and get groceries and such today," I reminded him. I hoped Carolyn could get a start on her task list, too.

-26- May 7$^{th}$ (Friday), Tucson, AZ

Taking advantage of my un-escorted state, and assuming it was only temporary, I went over to George's service station to see how things were going. They were going very well.

The truck had been unloaded and its load was stacked on pallets around the printing press behind the garage. The load turned out to consist of hundreds of copper rods, a long coil of pencil-lead-thick copper wire, and a solid stack of aluminum plates. We had about two thousand pounds of each type of stock.

What I came to see in particular was the truck. The green International DS-35 flatbed truck now looked the spitting image of a red DS-50. The auto body man contracted for the job was happy to have some work, no questions asked. Not much work was available when hardly anybody was driving, and half the vehicles on the road were flat army green. Without a tape measure one would have to be an expert to pick out the foot-shorter truck as an imposter.

George Zografos came out to meet me. "Nick! Good to see you. I have a buyer now for the aluminum. No luck on the copper yet, but don't we have a good offer from the big company yet?"

"No, they still think they're running the show," I explained. "I just shook off two of their men this morning."

"I see. So, tell me again what you want to do with this truck. We're going to make them think we have both of their special trucks, yes?"

"That's right. We can't pull it off for too long, but if we can get them to panic, they might settle up quickly." I looked the fake truck up and down. "I'd like to see us all get paid by the end of next week."

That was a satisfactory point to end on for George. He agreed that Stefano would go with me to San Diego to 'show' the truck at Zelatoff's secret facility, and to deal with whoever we met there.

"We only just got rid of two prisoners!" George complained. But he agreed that it was best to detain any other Zelatoff men until the deal was done. "So when do we take the truck over?"

"Tuesday afternoon we should be there. The real red truck should be on the road then, out of contact with anyone for a while." It would also give Carolyn just enough time to pass out my other invitations to the same party.

I asked for an escort back to my place to stash my car and a ride over to the fire station. George volunteered August for the job. I drove to my motel, stopping at the front office to ask about the two new men in the first cabin on the left. The manager volunteered that they were still checked in and he hadn't seen their car all morning. He wasn't comfortable sharing any other information, so I let him be and went back to my place.

August waited while I cleaned out my car and finished packing the bag I had prepared. I considered keeping the Night Eye machine to use after everything settled out, but I thought about all the interrogations that were sure to happen in the aftermath. I decided it would help my "good guy" image to turn in the secret machine. The pillow case would go with us to San Diego. I would keep the battery pack.

I looked back at my car as we pulled out of the motel. I hated leaving it alone, and felt vulnerable without it standing ready to get me in and out of trouble. I had my small guns with me, a couple changes of clothes, and my wits.

August surprised me by talking as soon as we got going in his car. "If you're going to the fire station, you should just take the truck."

"Is it ready to go?" I asked.

"I'll have it ready in no time if we go back to the garage. Your professor friend will be expecting it today." That mention put me at ease. I agreed to drive the truck over.

We got back to the garage and August finished getting the truck ready. He used the shop's small forklift

228

to stack some old wooden crates on the truck bed. When they added up to look like a substantial load he strapped everything down and checked me out on the machine.

He talked me through the shift pattern and showed me where to let air out of the rear tires. "At a quick look someone will think it's heavily loaded," he explained. With only a modest few jerks I got the truck rolling and started the few miles east to the closed fire station.

The station was of newer construction, a solid official building adorned in the style of 'good municipal budget year'. The textured face brick was of a custom color and features in the wall were capped with cut stones brought in from somewhere else. It was a good building, it just wasn't needed then and there. Besides the regional fire service being short-staffed, the Army had taken over much of the east part of greater Tucson, and all the responsibility for firefighting.

I brought the long truck around behind the station on its generous paved apron. Professor Arthur was there and expecting the truck. He opened the right of two bay doors and motioned me to bring the truck in.

With the truck inside, the office and shop areas of the building were to my right. To the left was an old fire truck. It wasn't an antique, like they bring out for parades, it was just older than most engines the department had by then. The old engine was no show piece. It was sitting on stout wooden blocks, the wheels and tires being elsewhere. It was also stripped of hoses and had been cannibalized for some of its fittings.

"They told us to economize on rubber and hardware," hollered the professor from my right, observing me looking at the old pumper truck.

I climbed down from my truck and followed him into the other half of the station. The inside had every facility of a fire station, besides a dormitory. It was a volunteer department so no one actually lived there.

A public facing counter was just inside the front door, three semi-private offices behind it. A short hallway led to a small meeting room and a larger class room behind that.

We walked into the very rear of the building, with a small kitchen and lounge, restroom, and the equipment storage locker. The locker was empty except for two folding cots and a small table. An improvised wire mesh wall had been added allowing access from the cage to the restroom. The only access into the space was through a solid door from the kitchen, secured by a pair of recently installed bolt locks.

"Are you sure you don't want to stay at my place?" the professor asked.

"No, you've done enough," I finally admitted. "Besides, I'm a hot property. I think I shook them for now, but I'd hate for any of this to follow you home." I looked around the little prison. "It looks like you've done a nice job here anyway. It's just like home."

"We need to find you someplace better to live," the professor said through a laugh. I put down my bag and we sat down in the little kitchen to catch up on the whole situation.

230

"Are you hungry?" I was asked. There was plenty of food left there so Arthur fixed us supper while I talked. I told him about the records that came in the mail, what I had asked Carolyn to do, and about losing the men sent to follow me.

"What about George?" he asked. "Won't he be pretty sore when you give up the whole game and no one's been paid?"

"I'm convinced that no one is ever getting paid. The man they brought in is a contract killer, even if he doesn't sell himself that way." I accepted a cup of coffee from my host. "There's an outside chance we can get paid for the load, and maybe for our trouble if we ask nicely. But the priority right now is to get this gang of thugs cleaned up before someone else gets hurt."

"Someone like you?" He looked back at me from the stove top.

"I'm about fifth on my list of concerns right now." I remembered something, "Hey, weren't you the first one to tell me to dig into this mess?"

He gestured at himself with a wet wooden spoon. "I wouldn't try to tell you to do anything." He did admit, "I may have encouraged you to consider the matter."

"In that case I'm up to fourth on that list." I got up to find the plates to set the table. "You just might have it coming."

We ate, cleaned up, and said goodbye for the night.

The tables had been turned on me. I was then sitting in the jail we had made for others. I was effectively confined there. The professor had his own life to catch up on, for appearances if not to keep up his little incomes. I didn't want to be seen around town, and certainly couldn't take out the Zelatoff truck when Nigel Thompson's men were looking for it.

The station had an old floor-standing radio. I let it run all evening and most of Saturday. The repetition of certain recordings was numbing. I was almost convinced to sell the truck and sink all the proceeds into war bonds.

I made up my mind to punch Kate Smith if we ever met. I wasn't on good terms with Bob Hope either.

The professor checked in on me Saturday afternoon. He brought me a stack of local newspapers, and a few from out of town. We talked about nothing, from baseball to labor strikes to old cars and new guns.

He left me a home cooked meal, from a recipe his wife used to make. I never thought to ask how long he'd been a widower.

After a couple hours he left. He had an afternoon class to teach at the gun club.

Late Monday morning Stefano came. Professor Arthur arrived later in his old pickup truck. He directed us in converting the fire station back to the way it had been.

We removed the new door bolts. He found some paint left over from construction of the young building. We used it after patching the walls where the steel mesh wall partition had been fastened.

The cots would stay one more day.

When the professor was satisfied he left us. Stefano would stay there and we would take the flatbed truck out late that night.

Finally, I had some real entertainment. Stefano shared stories from the old days, driving speed boats at night trying to beat the police craft (and usually winning).

His most colorful stories were the ones about Jersey shore tourists. Some would get seasick after five minutes on the calmest water. One fellow panicked when a three-foot wave splashed some water up onto the deck of his tour boat. The man jumped overboard into the chop and it took his boat and another to haul in the flailing land-lubber.

We ate from what was left in the station kitchen. We cleaned up, discarded the remaining food, and collected trash into a can the professor could collect on his final visit.

We laid down around nine p.m. Our alarm was set for 2 a.m. In the dark Stefano mused out loud, "Would it not be funny, Nick, if we met real bandits on the road? They would try to take a stolen truck with an empty cargo!"

I hadn't considered the possibility, but it was very real. We would run close to the border for most of the night. "What will you tell the bandits if we meet them, Stefano? They will not be very happy."

He laughed. "I sawed down my shot gun so I can use it from the truck cab. You have your pistol?" I said I did. "Then that is all we will tell them." The matter was closed and we slept.

The alarm sounded. We performed the required tasks and left. We took the long way around Tucson, away from most artificial light. I entertained dreadful thoughts, from my car and home being torn apart to Zelatoff men with Night Eye viewers on every road out of Tucson, waiting to pounce on us.

My mind calmed as we settled into the monotonous trek across the southern Arizona reservations. At 45 miles per hour vigilance was required even on the dullest straights. The truck was not built for exploring the wild night – it's headlights would give only short notice of a stubborn animal in the road. One poorly placed coyote could cause us serious grief.

Eventually we came up onto the main U.S. federal highway. We made good time through Yuma and the irrigated desert around El Centro but soon slowed to the official speed limit or less. The highway narrowed as it climbed into the southern California mountain ranges.

I kept in the lower gears as I worked the truck around dark turns and into deep valleys. Each bridge seemed to float over an infinite black abyss. I remembered that Sam Windham had met his end at one of those bridges, his assassin intending for him to find the ultimate bottom of the chasm.

By dawn we were headed mostly downhill. The passes opened and the road got wider. I kept our speed low. We had plenty of time and greater San Diego was busy enough that local police could still find profit in patrolling for speeding tickets at the edge of the metropolis. We were traveling in a stolen truck, as well, of a color that did not match its registration papers.

## -27- May 11<sup>th</sup> (Tuesday), San Diego, CA

We got off the main highway after clearing the last mountains. We meandered through the mixed neighborhoods on winding roads. Exclusive private communities shared address blocks with western style trailer parks and the occasional estate house of an old money San Diego socialite.

It was a perfectly pleasant midmorning when I took us into an industrial part of National City, where a big cargo truck would not look out of place parked on the street. I asked Stefano if he was hungry. He was looking across at a roadside place that was just getting set up to serve a line of waiting workmen. "It is never too early for a good burrito," he declared.

We waited in the line and put in an order. Stefano had sense to bring extra napkins back to the truck. The food was good, and messy, and of excessive quantity. We both nearly fell asleep in the cab as the morning sun moved to high noon.

When my watch said 12:30 I started the truck and we got moving again. I thought about what Carolyn might have been able to get done in the previous four days. My instructions to her had been to proceed no matter what. Whoever she did or didn't convince to play along would or would not show up at the appointed time.

We drove along the harbor front all the way to the north end. I stopped a block out from the back side of Universal Spline & Coupler. Stefano got out and pretended to inspect our load while I walked around to the alley between the buildings.

I got behind Universal and looked over the utility hook-ups. Everything had been painted over, and not recently. Only one old phone wire came out through the wall to the utility box. Nothing looked like a freshly installed line that might be tied to a monitored security system.

Stefano was dropping pressure from the rear tires as I rounded the corner again. The tires bulged a little, as intended. We got back in the truck and I pulled it around to park in front of Universal's front door. The truck's lights were left flashing and again Stefano got up to fuss over the load. Any casual onlookers would be distracted away from the man hunched over the building door lock.

It was a very conventional lock, and not new. They probably hadn't changed it after renting the space. I looked once more for any sign of an alarm installation and got busy raking the pins.

In four strokes I got the cylinder to tick toward me just slightly. I kept up tension as I brought up the lever from my pick kit to turn it. The lock turned easily and the door was open.

I stepped in and closed the door behind me. I walked to the right and found the chain for the big bay door. My first two pulls did nothing. I fumbled in the dark to find the sliding bolt holding the rolling door. I slid the bolt and pulled the chain again. The door ran up into its case and Stefano had the truck lined up to bring it in.

I closed the bay door behind the truck. Stefano thought to turn on the truck's lights for a moment while I found the room lights. I got them on. He shut down the truck and got out.

The room was exactly as Carolyn had described it, with little else to add. The workbenches, phones, shelves, and idle machine tools sat where she had described them. The only material addition was a small restroom in the far left corner of the shop, next to the row of heavy duty shelving.

I went over to the phones. As described one had a regular dial, the other only a single row of colored buttons on the otherwise conventional base. I scrounged around the work area and came up with a strip of fine sandpaper tape. It would suit my needs well as I worked to crank start the security machine at Zelatoff.

A switch box with just two options sat between the two phones. I turned the oversize knob toward the special phone and picked up its handset. I heard a conventional dial tone. I pressed the first button. The earpiece went silent as a pre-set number was clicked off.

A female voice answered, "Station one. Yes?" I rubbed the sandpaper several times over the perforated mouthpiece, mimicking bad electrical noise and static on the lines. "Hello?? Can you hear me?" I heard. I sent more noise and hung up. I tried the second button. A dozen rings came back and no one answered.

I tired the third button. A familiar man's voice said only, "Go." I sent through several rounds of noise. No response came. Nigel Thompson simply hung up.

Stefano was tinkering with the equipment on the shelves in back. I told him, "We'll have more company soon, probably just one man at first. We need to figure out where to hide so he can call in about the truck before we jump him."

We were still talking about hiding places and angles of control in the room when I heard a key in the front door.

I ran around behind the big machine tool, the one still in its wooden crate. Stefano dove his substantial mass under the truck bed and crawled to the far side.

A stout man in a flat gray suit came in and closed the door behind him. First he looked up at the high ceiling, puzzled that the room lights were on. Then his gaze came down and he froze in place, gaping at the red-bodied flatbed truck in front of him.

The man was known as Smiles. I had met him in Phoenix along with Harvey "Slim" Hackett. I peeked out from behind my box to see Stefano peeking back at me from behind the truck's right front wheel. I motioned at him palm-down to wait there and keep things on ice. He nodded and adjusted his squat to a more comfortable position.

Smiles walked up and down the length of the truck. I held my breath hoping he would not walk around the vehicle to Stefano's side. He turned and walked briskly over to the work benches. He poked into several cubby-holes under the bench top, coming out with a short crow bar in his pudgy hand.

Smiles loosened the front-most cargo strap on the truck. With some effort he clambered up onto the truck bed. He went to pry open one of the smaller crates, but it moved before he got real leverage on his tool. He picked up the crate and spun it around, feeling the light heft of the empty box.

He put the box down and pried again on the lid, holding the box still with a foot. He got the lid completely off to verify that it did indeed keep all of nothing from spilling out of the box.

He dropped the tool loudly onto the truck bed. He kicked a couple other boxes to check that they, too, were empty. He climbed down from the bed and went directly to the phones.

I switched sides of my hiding spot to continue spying on the hapless goon. He checked the switch box, picked up the handset of the special phone, and pressed the third button. He had skipped any intermediaries and gone directly to Mr. Thompson. I was delighted.

"Hey, chief. You're not going to believe this. The truck is here already, only it's empty and nobody else is here. What? No, I didn't try to call nobody else. I just got here." He paused to listen a moment. "Yeah, only there's crates on it but they're all empty. Yes, I'm sure it's our truck. The Night Eye is in the front seat." He listened again. "Yeah, yeah, I'll wait here."

Smiles hung up and turned around to look again at the red truck. He saw me and Stefano, guns leveled at his gut. He looked back and forth at each of us twice before he slowly raised his hands. We bound Smiles to a stool with electrical wire.

We looked over some of the hardware on the back shelves. Behind rows of standard battery packs were a variety of complicated vision systems.

Smiles talked freely, as was his custom. "Those are all prototypes they say. You should see the new ones, what the Army gets. They aren't half as big. You could wear one all night. It's all hush-hush stuff, but the Army loves 'em."

I kept the conversation going. "I bet they do. Is the whole thing made by Zelatoff?"

Smiles grinned wide, "That's the only way Mister Zelatoff likes it! Plus, since it's all secret the Army likes it that way too. So what are you here for, Nick?"

He remembered my name, and his curiosity deserved an answer. "I'm just here to collect what's coming to me. Your boss made a fool of me and I need my name back. I'll take cash if that's on offer too."

"You want to get paid?" He looked back and forth at Stefano and me. "I don't think mister Z is going to be very happy when he gets here. He won't be handing out money, I don't think."

"Wait, Penko Zlatkov is coming here!?" When I had referred to Smiles' boss, I meant Thompson. Zlatkov had said Thompson took care of everything, leaving him hands-off of the dirty business, and I had believed him. I never dreamed I could lure the old man out of his office.

Smiles finally realized he'd said too much. He looked down at his bounds. "Now, don't go getting too excited, Nick. I don't know who else is coming and I don't want any trouble to start while I'm tied up and can't duck bullets."

I told Smiles to relax, that I had it covered. Stefano didn't show it, but he too had to be concerned about what entourage our VIP guest might bring.

I took him to the far corner of the room and leveled with him about who else I expected to show up on our team. He wasn't entirely pleased about that news, either, but I swore he had nothing to worry about. He also had no choice.

We waited quietly for a while. A few minutes before four I unlocked the front door and stepped outside. I walked across to the north side of the street and leaned up against the facing building to smoke a slow cigarette.

The cigarette was nearly out the next time I checked my watch. At six minutes after four a blue sedan turned onto the quiet street a quarter mile to the east. It approached to within a block of my position and parked.

The car was driven by a man I would come to learn was Ross Malick. Behind him sat Carolyn Barnes. Next to him was an older man I had not met nor spoken to. I looked both ways along the street and waved them on.

All three people got out of the car and walked briskly toward Universal. I opened the door and let us all in.

Stefano stood twenty feet in from the door, shotgun ready held across his waist. I closed half the distance toward the wary Greek as the others filed in behind me. "These are the people I was expecting. They're on our side, you can relax."

The new man spoke up, "Don't be so sure about that just yet!" I turned my head and raised an eyebrow toward at the man. I hoped he wouldn't say anything else to irritate Stefano.

I turned to face him and crossed my arms. He was surveying our bound prisoner when I asked, "OK, then. Let's start with who you are and what it is you need to know."

Ross Malick spoke up. "Nick, this is John Dewey, detective with San Diego County; good to meet you by the way. I showed him what we have on your 'Jack'."

The older man reached into his over-weight gray suit jacket and pulled out a business card to stick in my face. J. Anders Dewey was listed on the heavy card stock.

Detective Dewey spoke for himself, "If you can show me who killed Samuel Windham, I'd be obliged. In the meantime, I'm going to have to ask why you have a man tied up here."

I asked Malick if Dewey knew about the upside-down smuggling ring. Carolyn interjected that only the other people she'd talked to had heard about all that. I looked at my watch wondering if those other people were going to show up in time. Zlatkov and Thompson could be on us any minute if they had left Palm Springs right away.

I told Carolyn to watch the street through a hole she would scratch in the window paint. I darkened the room again and proceeded to convince the detective to be patient with us a bit longer.

I tried to summarize for him the whole scheme and how I thought it had got Windham killed. He hmm'ed through my story, but stayed focused on his own job. "So this Jacques fellow, is he coming here? I can have deputies waiting for him."

I wasn't going to convince Dewey that our fish were bigger than his. I assured him that we had enough muscle, official and otherwise, to handle whoever showed. I still wondered if the other official muscle was going to show.

We didn't have long to wait before Carolyn called out, "Car coming, from the left. I don't think it's one of ours." She kept looking. "It stopped at the corner. Two men getting out, that's all. One has a cane."

We all moved to hasty hiding spots, covering us from the door. Stefano and I carried Smiles in his chair to a spot behind the truck cab. Stefano leaned down close to Smiles' face and with a gesture to his lips warned the talkative man to stay quiet.

The door swung open in a blink. I had left it unlocked. The silhouette of Nigel Thompson filled the door frame. He took two steps into the dark room, pausing to draw his gun and scan the empty space in front of him.

He turned to wave in the man behind him. Penko Zlatkov stepped through the door and closed it. Thompson found the lights and switched them on.

I watched the legs of the men from under the back of the flat bed. They observed the truck for a long moment. Thompson said something quietly and turned toward the phones. He took two steps in that direction and Zlatkov turned to follow.

On that cue I slipped out from behind the truck, Stefano right behind me. I ran up behind the men, stopping ten feet away with my pistol aimed through the middle of Thompson. Stefano moved to my left, between the men and the door. For good measure Malick aimed his piece over the hood of the truck.

Smiles finally found his courage to speak up from behind the truck, "Boss, look out!" It was too late, and Smiles' courage faded in front of Carolyn, who was holding the revolver I'd given her up to his right eyeball.

Thompson didn't flinch, didn't reach into his jacket, didn't do anything fast or dumb. He turned slowly, raising his hands to shoulder height. Zlatkov watched Thompson and followed his lead.

Malick holstered his gun and came over to disarm Thompson. He frisked both men. "I'm sorry, sir," he addressed Zlatkov. "We'll find you a comfortable place to sit," he said as he relieved the man of his expensive walking stick.

The broad shouldered Zlatkov stood up straight as a chimney and walked stiffly toward the work benches. He picked up a shop stool, brought it back to the middle of the room, and declared, "I will do just fine with one of these."

I motioned for Carolyn to go back to her window post. We got the prisoners arranged in the center of the room again. The county detective surveyed our haul and spoke up, "I suppose these are the two you told me about," he said to me without addressing me.

He moved to stand in front of Nigel Thompson. "How about your man Jacques Tourel? Did you call him here?"

Thompson had no reaction. "Why should I call anyone? I only stopped here to check on a bad phone line."

Dewey turned toward Zlatkov, still speaking to Thompson. "And what about your boss here, does he come along on every phone repair job?" It wasn't right for the detective to be interrogating *my* prisoners, but I had to leave him something to do.

Thompson had answered questions like this before. "We had other business in town. You can check with the lawyers. This was on our way back."

"More cars," called out Carolyn from the front wall. "Army. I think they're ours, and they're making a lot of fuss."

-28- May 11th (Tuesday), San Diego, CA

I ran to the door and stepped outside to look. From the west two Army MP cars were rolling down the street with strobe lights turning.

I stepped out into the street to wave them off, away from right in front of Universal Spline & Coupler. It didn't help.

The cars split up to either side of the street. One stopped just short of Universal's bay door and the other directly across the street from the front window. Each car disgorged four men – five soldiers, two officers, and one dark-suited man in total.

They didn't know me or care who I was. Two of the soldiers took positions either side of me. The others lined up with their detail commander in front of the building.

To the west I saw more movement. Another car was approaching. A stubbornly brown little sedan drew nearer tentatively. The intractably ugly visage of Jacques Tourel came into focus. He stopped his car at the intersection before Universal. He fixed a look on me that I will never forget, smiled in his inimitable sneer, and turned his car up the cross street, away from the trap that had nearly caught him. He was gone.

I turned to see where the men in charge of the newly arrived circus had got to. The man in the suit and the senior officer were standing behind me. "I'm Nicolas Guyon," I told them. "You came here on my account."

I looked around at the soldiers and flashing military police cars. "It's all over. Everything is settled inside. It'd be best if we went in quietly, just the three of us." The officer of the detachment, a young lieutenant, got his men to stand down and check their rifles. I motioned the other men to go on inside.

As they stepped toward the building I noticed another man on the street. All by himself, on the next block to the east, a man was smoking a cigarette by a sign post. He seemed unaffected by the show we had put on. It was August, George Zografos' man, sent to keep an eye on my operation.

I was reminded of everything I had to get accomplished in the next few minutes. I still hoped to both stay out of prison and make good with George and his team.

We all got inside and a round of introductions was made, including the seated prisoners.

The new man in the suit was even younger than I thought at first. He identified himself as Mr. Shockey of the Federal Bureau of Investigation. He did not say "agent" of the FBI. Carolyn tugged on my sleeve. I leaned down for her to whisper, "He's Bobby, the best I could do on short notice."

The senior Army officer was Colonel Robert Janney, an Army buyer for 'special' projects. "It's a wonder you found me, but I'm glad, if half of what she told me is true."

Carolyn answered, "It's all true. And we found you through their own lawyers. They had a practice going of suing the government over contract issues. Some of the suits are over contracts for secret equipment. They're blacked out all over, but they show up like pink elephants for what all is missing from the files. The details are all sealed, but they can't leave out the named parties, and they called you out by name twice."

The colonel nodded appreciatively at the leg work, but was probably already thinking about how to close that peephole.

"The business of secrets has its odd ends, for sure," he mused. "The second time Zelatoff filed to replace stolen material the production resources board came to ask me about it. I agreed that we couldn't make too big a fuss without exposing top-secret programs to a lot of outsiders." On that thought he looked around the room at the mob assembled there. "Not much of what Zelatoff said went missing was earmarked for my equipment, but once the investigation starts a complete accounting would have to be done."

The county detective had been quiet for longer than I guessed was customary for him. "Is all we're going to talk about some stolen lumps of scrap metal?

Someone has been killed over this and I need the killer!"

"He's right outside," I told the old cop. "Or he was before the cavalry showed up ringing church bells to announce their arrival. Last I saw he turned up 28$^{th}$ toward downtown. That was twenty minutes ago."

He detective huffed and hummed, looked at several faces in the group, and stomped over to the phones. "Turn the switch to the left," I instructed him, "then dial straight out."

Colonel Janney had gone to the door to have a couple of the MPs sent in. He came back to the huddle and addressed me. "Mr. Guyon, the people held here are suspected of federal crimes." He looked to the FBI man who nodded. "Considering the other national defense issues involved, I'm going to ask that they be put into military custody for the time being." Mr. Shockey had no objections.

Penko Zlatkov did, standing up to insist, "Damn you, Janney. You still don't know what you're doing. You wouldn't take reasonable terms for the Night Eyes, and now you won't have any. It will not be made without me." Zlatkov was quickly winded. He sat again and continued, "As Mr. Thompson said, we were only just speaking with my lawyers. They could save you a great deal of trouble if you speak to them now."

I didn't doubt that they had prepared a plan with the lawyers for just this eventuality, a thick folder of cover stories, plausible excuses, and procedural maneuvers. Mr. Thompson for his part would have drilled his men on how to lie and when to vanish should the scheme break down. Protecting Zlatkov would have been easier if Zlatkov had not been in the thick of it the whole time.

The 50-something colonel had his share of gray hairs from dealing with Zlatkov's lawyers. He was not going to invite more. "Invoking some executive order that I'll look up later," he knew there were plenty to pick from, "you're going to be held in military custody and you'll talk to your lawyers yourself, later, after I dig through their files myself."

Nigel Thompson tried to make himself useful. "You listen here," he said from his stool, "you can't just throw on a rank and start barking out orders wherever you want! If the FBI man here thinks there's a criminal case, this is his turf." He was looking at Shockey, hoping for an unlikely ally.

Colonel Janney let the proposition float. "What about it, Mr. Shockey? That pile of secret hardware in the back is supposed to be locked up, if not destroyed by now. Does that sound like something you want to look into?"

"Honestly," the young man admitted, "taking a case over military secrets is always a royal pain for the agents and prosecutors. If you've got a way to keep me out of this, I'm for it." I wondered if the FBI clerk, or whatever he really was, was even supposed to be there.

I cut in, remembering the rest of my own agenda. I asked Colonel Janney if I could see him outside, with Ross Malick. As we walked out I heard Detective

Dewey still on the phone with his office, "The Tourel file! Yes, it should be right there on my desk. Well where did it get to then? Just find it, and get that picture out!"

We stepped out into the pleasant afternoon day. The industrial street took an odd sort of pastoral feel as the breeze tossed a few stray leaves up into the lowering sun. Only a pair of ugly army cars, three bored soldiers smoking cheap cigarettes, and knowledge of the odd circus inside could spoil the scene.

Ross Malick was about five years older than me, but in better health. His clean tan skin showed on his neck up to a neatly trimmed brown hair line under a hat with a wider flatter brim than most people wore any more. His suit was well cut but had been worn for more than a few long days. The new shoes under it had comfortable soft soles, the style popular with 'gumshoes.'

The colonel said some unpleasant things about Zlatkov's mother then asked what I wanted to talk about. "But before you start," he continued, "let me tell you how much we appreciate this. We're just not set up to look after outfits like this, and the FBI can't keep up either. OK, shoot."

"I'm glad you appreciate it, because Malick and I are out some significant time and we have some expenses." Janney nodded without comment. "Plus, there's the matter of the last load of metal. I might have promised the men helping me they could sell it."

The colonel waved off any concern, "Oh, that? That's easy. I've had cargoes with my stuff on it insured at above-official rates. Since prices are controlled that's probably illegal, but it gets my stuff replaced faster if it gets lost. Write me a receipt and I can buy the whole lot."

I glanced up the street to the east. August was no longer there watching us. I would have run over yelling the good news if he was. Instead I bit my lip.

Ross Malick picked up the ball and kept running. "The boys will appreciate that. But that leaves us two with weeks of work into it. Can you cover that?"

"Well now," Janney thought for a second, "personnel costs are a different department. I can buy things, but to hire people... OK, could you just figure out your expenses and round it up, way up? If you write up a list I can pay it out of the running budget. It's not like I'll be paying Zelatoff invoices for a while."

Bureaucracy is an odd and beautiful thing sometimes.

Our immediate business settled Janney went back to directing the MPs. Carolyn and Stefano came outside to find us. Malick wanted to make dinner plans. Carolyn had to get back to her children. Of course the children were invited.

I told Stefano that we were going to get paid after all. He went inside to call George in Tucson, since August probably already had done the same. Malick asked if we needed a ride back to Tucson. I said

Stefano and I would be all right if we caught up with August.

He said he was already going to miss me when I got my practice going in Tucson. My thoughts then were only of packing my things into my car and moving on again.

I smelled the cool breeze and took another look at the downtown skyline north of us. It shone calmly in the warm afternoon sun. "No, I think I'll stay here for a while."

# Epilogue

Penko Zlatkov stayed true to his word. The Night Eye machine was never made again. He and Thompson never faced charges, but Zlatkov was kept in custody for almost a year and never allowed back into his own office. His whole company dissolved quickly without him, like it had swallowed a poison pill.

Key people retired or simply stopped showing up to work. The most critical tools broke mysteriously. Technical drawings needed to replace them went missing. The government took over the entire operation but couldn't force it to remain an instrument of their plans. The company's R&D shop closed up in six months for lack of scientists and technicians to pursue even the existing projects.

The concept of what came to be generically called "night vision" equipment was passed to other companies but their engineers had to start from scratch. They got a limited number of crude devices into service too late to make a difference in the war.

Nicolas Guyon stayed on in San Diego, keeping Carolyn with him. I don't get to talk to him much anymore, and I'm not unhappy for that. I've had plenty of excitement in my time. At the last I heard he was being lauded for busting up an ugly human smuggling operation.

I went back to teaching history after the war. I built a whole course around the transformation of America at home during the global conflict. Some of the 'real' faculty complained about me teaching 'history' out of events that only just happened.

I reminded them that history doesn't happen on a convenient time-table. It happens every day, sometimes in great leaps, right on top of us, whether we recognize it or not.

- *"Professor" Arthur Mason, MFA*

## From the Author

Thank you for reading my book.

If you might do another favor to me, and to other prospective readers, please consider leaving a review at your favorite online retailer or reader community. If the novel did not meet your expectations, please be clear about what could have been different on the cover or back matter to better describe the work.

Nick Guyon will be back. Keep in touch at sdmahaney.org for updates on new work. And you never know when an online-only short story may appear.

www.ingramcontent.com/pod-product-compliance
Lightning Source LLC
Chambersburg PA
CBHW021958170626
46808CB00001B/207